The Face in the Flames

Les Ireland

The Face
in the Flames

Matador
12 Manor Walk, Coventry Road
Market Harborough
Leics LE16 9BP, UK
Tel: (+44) 1858 468828 / 469898
Fax: (+44) 1858 431649
Email: books@troubador.co.uk
Web: www.troubador.co.uk/matador

ISBN 1-904744-10-9

Typeset in 10pt Plantin Light by Troubador Publishing Ltd, Market Harborough, UK
Printed and bound by TBA

Matador is an imprint of Troubador Publishing

For Lucy, Corin and Leah

1

Teon sobbed. The small figure, hands still tied behind his back, squatted in the corner and cried. His shoulders shook, the tears dripped onto his tunic, his sobs echoed against the stone. Long hours ago he had lost any real sense of feeling in those hands. Teon hadn't cried before. Now he was sitting on the damp floor in the dark cell, many many miles from home, his desolation sweeping over him. And even worse – no-one heard him. His own people had abandoned him. His own father couldn't help him. His own people now only a memory – did they ever exist? The only voices he could hear were the two guards, laughing, arguing, drinking, as they played cards at the end of the corridor on which the door of his cell opened.

Teon noticed nothing of his cell. Even the deep booming clang of the cell door being slammed had hardly penetrated his senses. The damp bare stone floor flecked with moss and lichen; The tiny window high on the wall allowing a dribble of light into the cell, pushed in by the cold draught; the lonely bucket in the corner – there was nothing else in the cell: Teon had noticed none of it. It was dark when he had been brought here, and the corridor along which he had been led was poorly lit. The cell was in almost total darkness. There would have been little to see had he been aware of his surroundings, but his despair had deepened through the afternoon and he had noticed nothing by sight or touch. He was not even aware of the blood on his feet from the walking. He was not aware of the rope burns on his wrists, nor his hunger, though he had not eaten since that morning. Now – there were only tears left.

For a moment Teon's sobs halted and the voices in the corridor penetrated his mind, but the voices made it all feel worse as they spoke in a harsh and rough tongue – he knew it was the same tongue as he spoke but he could not make sense of what they said. The alien voices of his guards made him feel even more alone, even more distant from home, and the tears, the sobs, the gut-wrenching loneliness swept over him with renewed vigour. He had not felt like this even when his mother died four years before. Then Teon had wanted to die: now he did not even have that much spirit left: the sobbing, the exhaustion, the emptiness of his stomach sapped all the energy he had, the pain in his wrists and feet doing nothing more than keeping him from sleep.

Seven days before the great visitation had taken place – the leaders of the Bayronites had come to Teon's country. The royal party was led by the Emperor – he was called Pellaig but no-one used his name: such was his power and standing that he was simply called "The Emperor" both in his own land and in neighbouring lands as well. He had ruled his people with a cold face and iron fist for over thirty years, thirty years of prosperity and security.

The royal party also included many of his nobles, his elite bodyguard troops, his entire court. All had made the visit to Teon's country – Fethon. Bayron neighboured Fethon to the east and felt rather like the big domineering neighbour over the border, and in the minds of the Fethonites had always felt threatening. That was the reason for the visit: the King of the Fethonites, Jayron – had wanted to build peace and had invited the Emperor of the Bayronites to visit.

Jayron had been king now for 2 years, and as young as he was – he was 24 when he had come to the throne – he was known as a man for the people. A man of peace. A man of insight. His Father had been a true man, a man's man, and favourite of the people – he had been lively, fun, loved, respected, a man of great energy and generosity. When he died – he had collapsed at the party after one of his many hunting trips – the nation had mourned: the king had felt like a favourite uncle to his people. Jayron was very different – quiet, thoughtful, with eyes that penetrated right into your heart when he was talking to you. Talk to Jayron and you felt, for those few moments, that you were the only person who existed. That Jayron had heard everything you said. That Jayron knew exactly what was going on in your mind, and heart, and soul. At first people had said he was half the man his father was. He had never enjoyed hunting, never even attended parties, rather spent his time learning music. His people had laughed cynically – what use would it be to have a king who was virtuoso on the column, their ancient form of violin? Already, barely two years later, people were saying that Jayron would be the greatest king the nation had ever known, such was the wisdom, justice and peacefulness he brought to the role of king.

At first people had mistaken Jayron's peacefulness for weakness, but he had proved his strength and courage many times in his dealings with neighbouring countries. His most famous encounter was with the southern Kento people who decided to ride north to conquer Fethon shortly after Jayron had taken power. Their army had numbered a thousand horsemen. Jayron took with him two hundred. They had faced each other on the battle field, when Jayron had dismounted from his horse, removed his weapons and walked alone straight towards the Kento. His own warriors were horrified – the risk he faced of capture or being killed.

Jayron had stopped twenty yards short of the Kento and began to speak them. He told them of their own history as a noble people. He told them of their honour as warriors. He told them how invading Fethon would give them no honour. He told them how important friendship was. He told them how nobility came from equal relationships, not exploiting the poor. His oratory was remarkable: soaring, crying, piercing, challenging, carrying all with him.

Jayron had known the nature of the Kento people. His own warriors were amazed to see the Kento army turn and return south, their leaders staying to cement a relationship and trade deals. The performance of Jayron went into legend – the king who turned an invasion with a speech.

The visit of the Bayronites had been tense – as much as Jayron of the Fethonites wanted peace, so the Emperor wanted to be seen as the regional leader, wanted Bayron to be the acknowledged regional superpower. He had taken a huge number of officials. Hundreds of soldiers. His entire court had accompanied him on the trip. For the King of Fethon it felt at times like an invasion and the expense of feeding and housing all these visitors had been huge.

The visit had not made the relationship between the two countries worse, although no real progress to an equal peace was made. For many of the Bayronites the visit had been thoroughly boring. The Bayronites felt the Fethonite court was too puritanical, too spartan, compared to the great parties they had been used to at the court in their own country. There had been simple food compared to what they were used to at the court at home in Gresk, the great capital city of Bayron. There was far less drink than they had enjoyed back in Bayron. Seven days of this had been so dull that the crown prince of the Bayron and only son of the Emperor – Hamlan – decided to return home early with a group of friends.

Six of the Bayronites, including Hamlam, rode home alone – they had grown thoroughly bored of Jayron who actually seemed to care for his people more than he cared for partying. To them Jayron was too self-sacrificing as he put the needs of his people first. Surely there was no point in being king if you didn't use the post to enhance your own quality of life? To put it simply, there hadn't been enough alcohol to drink. There hadn't been any women to chase. If it hadn't been for the Bayronite rum they had brought with them the trip would have been almost totally dry.

The small group left Durringham – Fethom's capital city – and rode eastwards all day until they reached the village of Mayeringham on the frontier of the two nations.

Mayeringham was a small frontier town with a population of about a hundred. It was a village that survived on trading and drink. A few of the residents bought cloth from Fethon and sold it in the markets of Bayron. They bought drink from the Bayronites and sold it to travellers between the two countries: What Mayeringham did best was provide taverns and guest houses for travellers. For many it was a good place to stop to get refreshed, to spend the night; for others it was no more than a shambles of huts to pass through quickly.

Mayeringham was known for two things. Firstly, it was known for the poverty of the people who survived there eking out a living in poor trade – there was little profit to be made in ale, and little demand for cloth. Mayeringham was made all the poorer as trade went up and down depending on the relationship between Fethon and Bayron, a relationship that had been decidedly rocky over the previous thirty years. There had been many times when the inhabitants of Mayeringham had to run and hide in the surrounding hills as the two countries had been at war, the village caught in the skirmishes and destroyed: many villagers once – eighteen years before – massacred when the raid had come too quickly. The villagers now were very much people who lived on the edge of both nations, despised by both. At the same time, however, Mayeringham was known for the level of hospitality the village gave: it could afford to turn away no-one, everyone was given a bed and food on their travels. Not that the people were naturally hospitable, but hospitality was part of their survival, their greatest source of income.

The leader of the village was an older man – Bohran. Bohran had served as an officer in the Fethonite army in his younger days before moving to Mayeringham to be village elder. He had been elder for many years – since the massacre, and had been a good leader in his earlier years, standing tall in his uniform, helping to rebuild the village, years when his ideals had still been intact. Now Bohran was tired, his back had become bent and his career in the civil service had progressed no further. Leading such a poor and desperate community had taken its toll: Bohran stayed more and more in his office attached to his home. It was whispered that he should stand down, but no-one had the courage to make it happen and to be honest no-one really wanted the job. Leading such a poor and despised community was a thankless task.

It was into this community that Hamlan and his friends came that night having left Durringham in the early morning. They came demanding rooms, the best rooms. Bohran briefly appeared from his office and sent the party to Hesteon who agreed – they could stay the night. Hesteon was a man of about 40, big built, muscular. He was happy to provide hospitality, but really eked out his existence as a builder, building the houses and shacks that made up Mayeringham. Many saw him as successor to Bohran as village elder, but Hesteon wanted the job as little as anyone else. He had lived all his life in Mayeringham, escaping the massacre by being away on army service at the time, but returning shortly after to help rebuild his community.

Although his home wasn't big, Hesteon took a pride in keeping it neat, making it comfortable, maintaining a good place to live. The home had four rooms – the sitting room in which Hamlan and his friends were now gathered, two bedrooms, one each for Hesteon and Teon, and the kitchen. The kitchen and the sitting room both had doors out into the yard, but the sitting room and bedrooms also had doors – rough wooden doors – into the kitchen. Hesteon himself had built the house.

For Hesteon keeping the house immaculate was a duty, a tribute. He had been deeply in love with Janci, a beautiful dark haired girl originally from the far west of Fethon. She had been passing through the village with her family, had met Hesteon and they had fallen in love overnight. She simply refused to leave the village; they had married within three days and in time Teon had been born. Janci had kept the house immaculately until, when Teon was about 11, she became very ill and, within days, had died. Hesteon and Teon themselves had dug the grave for her high on the hill above their village, the hill where they as a family would picnic in good weather. The cause of death was never known, but both Hesteon and Teon were distraught. With time they had adjusted, but Hesteon kept the house immaculate in tribute to the wife he had adored, and had lost. Hesteon was of Bayronite descent, although both he and his father and his father's father had been born in Mayeringham, their Bayronite roots mostly forgotten.

That evening Hesteon fed Hamlan as well as he could, but bread and cold meat are barely food for a prince. Hamlan was loud, brash and confident. He also demanded drink to accompany his meal – if he had to eat bread and meat, at least he would have something to taste beside it. All the way through the meal Hamlan drank a lot, then drank a lot more laughing with his friends through the evening, until around midnight he simply toppled over in his seat, and in seconds was snoring gently. Hamlan's friends took this as the cue to end the conversation and also lay down to sleep as well, the drink and the presence of the snoring prince forcing them to sleep themselves. Only one of them – Magrell, the young and ambitious commander of the Bayronite army, had kept off the drink. His mind was racing as the night closed around them.

After the party went to sleep, Hesteon washed the dishes and cleaned the rooms of his house. He was relieved. These occasions could get noisy and violent, but this time there had been no real trouble. He knew Hamlan would move on early next morning – quietened from the hangover, wanting to move out to get home as soon as possible. He was also angry, grumbling to Teon as they had washed the dishes, that he wouldn't get any payment for this expense – you never got paid when royalty stayed. Late in the night he and Teon went to their separate beds and were asleep in seconds.

"WHAT IS THIS?" A voice shouted from the room where Hamlan and his friends were sleeping. Hesteon and Teon were already up and working in the kitchen, preparing breakfast, although they hadn't dared enter the sitting room where the party spent the night. The voice was from one of Hamlan's friends – Hesteon thought from the one he had heard called Magrell. It was dawn: his shouting woke the other friends who had slept the sleep of the drunk, and even woke people in the next house. Hesteon and Teon hurried to the main room in response. The Bayronites were slowly rousing themselves out of the drink enhanced sleep.

On the floor lay one of the Bayronites, blood trickling from his mouth. His tunic was bright red, blood still seeping out of the body from inside the tunic. The red of the blood was spreading onto the floor. A sword handle showed on the chest of the man, the blade coming out through his back – someone had thrust the sword right through the man's heart as he had slept. The figure had no life; the only movement the blood still leaving his body and slowly spreading around him; the body was cold and still. Hamlan was barely recognisable, but was certainly and totally dead – killed by his own sword.

Within minutes the inhabitants of the village gathered around the front of Hesteon's house. The remaining Bayronites stood beside Bohran the village elder, his face now covered with fear, his back seemingly even more stooped than normal. Hesteon stood slightly behind them, Teon hidden, part of the crowd. Magrell was shouting at the people. Magrell stood tall, a commanding presence. He demanded that the culprit be found, that the killer be discovered and handed over to them. "It's like this" he had sneered. "At noon our army will be riding through here, returning to Bayron. If the culprit is not found, we will slaughter the whole village". As he spoke, his hand swept over the gathered crowd. Suddenly his tone changed to anger as he pointed to the crowd. "Not one of you will be left alive" he screamed. "The culprit must be found; the coward must step forward".

The crowd was silent. Totally silent for what seemed an age. The minds of the people were whirling. Teon was remembering life in the village. A typical lad of 15, yet to fill out, black hair never combed, easily embarrassed, he still enjoyed playing with his friends, helping his father, yet he enjoyed the country, the flowers. Some described him as sensitive. Others reckoned he was a good looking lad, would be a handsome man when older. Teon even enjoyed the village life, as poor as it was. He had great dreams of joining the Fethonite Army when he was old enough. Yet into this thought came other thoughts, screamed at him by this military commander, this stranger standing outside of Teon's house, his own house. The whole village killed. Everything gone. His own life cut short. Everything was about to end. The thoughts churned back and fore – his love of life, his fear of the Bayronites. His love for Fethon. For Mayeringham. His horror at what he had seen in the family home – he had been with his mother when she had died, but this was different – the blood, the brutality, the murder felt much harsher. For an age, or what seemed an age, the villagers and the Bayronites stood stunned in silence. No one moved. Occasionally Magrell demanded the culprit be given up. The culprit be handed over.

Inside Magrell smiled at the thought that only five Bayronites could cower all the villagers here. He smiled at the collective weakness of the villagers. He smiled as he saw the fear in their eyes, the fear engendered by what had happened, the fear at what Magrell said he would do to them.

Magrell seemed to be losing patience. He turned sharply to Hesteon. He spoke in a voice laden with sarcasm, just loud enough for everyone to hear. "Perhaps you", he pointed at Hesteon, "Have something you want to tell me".

Hesteon was silent for a moment, his mind a confusion of thoughts. Hesteon began to babble "I didn't do it, sir. Wouldn't want to harm anyone. Never entered the room sir..."

"QUIET." Magrell stopped Hesteon. Hesteon stopped speaking immediately. Magrell continued, his voice suddenly accusatorial "So you say, but you had every opportunity. Anytime through the night you could have done it. You had more opportunity than anyone else. And you have the look of a coward who would kill a man in his sleep." Magrell stopped, and spat on the ground in contempt.

"Is this yours?" Magrell produced a shirt covered with blood – it had hung conveniently in the kitchen.

Hesteon was quiet for moments, his face suddenly pale. He recognised the shirt as his own, one Gowli his neighbour had sown for his previous birthday. He had no idea how it was covered with blood. Hesteon mumbled: "I haven't worn it for months..."

Magrell spoke, his face inches from Hesteon's. "Answer the question, fool – is this your shirt?"

For a moment there was silence. It was Magrell who continued. "So this is your shirt. Do we need any further proof?"

Teon's mind was whirling even harder. His father accused. His father couldn't have done it; his father wasn't like that. His father had suffered enough in his life. His father didn't deserve this, to be humiliated like this in front of the villagers. Teon looked at his father, now cowering, a broken man in face of these accusations, in face of this man, the leader of the Bayronite army. Teon felt he couldn't, mustn't lose his father.

Again, Magrell's voice penetrated Teon's thoughts. This time Magrell was speaking to Bohran. "It's clear to me, Elder, that the guilty man is here". He gestured in Hesteon's direction. "Are you prepared for us to take the action that is necessary?"

This time it was Bohran who replied in a gabble. "Always found him to be honest, sir. Never thought he could do this, Sir. Never harmed anyone before sir..." Bohran's voice trailed away, partly cowered by the glare Magrell aimed towards him, partly out of relief – the dawning realisation he shared with the village that if Hesteon had done it he and the rest of the village would survive.

Again Magrell spoke harshly. "QUIET". Magrell turned to Hesteon, and stared hard and long towards him, before speaking coldly again. "Scum. You will come with us to Gresk. There you will be tried, and there..." He paused before continuing slowly and coldly. "...You will hang for everyone to see the coward you are..."

"I did it". Teon was only half aware of the voice – his voice. Then the thoughts came rushing. It was the only way to save the village. It was the only way to turn aside the Bayronites. The only way to turn aside this man in his anger. It was the only way to save all he loved. He could save his family. His friends. He hadn't even thought of consequences – wasn't even aware there might be consequences – he alone could save his village. His one over-whelming thought was to save his father – his father's reputa-tion, his father's honour, his father's life.

Teon was aware of all eyes looking at him. The silence was ear-shattering. It was broken by a villager's voice. "He couldn't have". Another said "not him". Another said: "he had the best chance". A hundred voices were raised as they doubted or wanted Teon to have done it. Only Hesteon remained silent, star-ing in shock, open-mouthed in horror at his son who had just stepped forward from the crowd.

As the moments passed Teon was only half aware of the uproar that was going on around him. There were the Bayronites demanding they took Teon to Gresk, their capital city, for justice. There was Bohran, agreeing, too weak in spirit to stop it happen-ing. There was Hesteon being held back by friends struggling to save his son. Then Teon was aware of the ropes around his arms, the stabbing pain as they were pulled tight, then released slightly. He was vaguely aware of a rope tied from his hands to a horse, of being made to walk beside a horse, urged on by a kick from the man on the horse, by Magrell. Two of the Bayronites – Magrell and another – decided to take Teon on ahead. The other three remained at the village until the rest of the returning Bayronites passed through to organise the return of Hamlan's body to his own city. Soon Teon was over the border, on the road to Gresk, capital of Bayron.

For Teon the journey seemed never ending. Even in his simple rough tunic and trousers he found himself getting very warm. He kept his eyes to the ground as he walked. The rocks were hard to his feet and easily cut through his thin leather sandals.

Sometimes he stumbled, each time to be dragged back to his feet with the rope. He walked. Sometimes he stood as the riders dismounted to take refreshment or to allow the horses to feed. Neither man said anything to Teon. Neither man took any notice of him. He wasn't given anything to eat or drink. His mind whirled in the mixture of pain in his feet, numbness in his arms, dryness of his throat, the heat on his head, the despair and dread in his heart. There seemed to be only the road and the horror of what was happening to him.

By the time they reached Gresk, the capital city of Bayron, towards mid evening, Teon knew nothing except the walking and the pain in his feet – his sandals were in tatters from the rock-strewn path. He was not even aware of the sun setting around them, the colder evening setting in. He was not aware of being taken into the city, then into the Emperor's palace, of being taken through dark passages, down steps into the ever colder lower levels of the palace. He was not even aware of the angry glares, the odd blows from soldiers who could get close enough – the tale of what he had done travelling through the palace more quickly than he could.

Finally Teon was put into the cell, dark, cold, with no food or furniture. And the sorrow, the tears, the pain in feet and arms, had all overtaken him. Only one thing now penetrated his despair. He kept remembering the voice of Magrell. Magrell had whispered sarcastically to him as he had left Teon in the cell. "Boy – your stupid sacrifice has saved me a lot of awkward questions..."

2

The villagers in Mayeringham were still reeling with the events of the day: overnight – literally – they had been faced with the awful dilemma. The shock of finding the Prince of the Bayronites murdered in their village. The fear that they were all to be butchered. The even greater shock of discovering that Teon had done it. The rationalisation – they had found Hamlan's purse missing, had heard how Teon knew they were not going to pay. They had concocted Teon's anger. The rest of the Bayronites had arrived, and quickly the situation had been explained. Four soldiers collected Hamlan's body from Teon's house and the Bayronites went on their way. By that evening the people of Mayeringham had returned to a semblance of normality, the villagers simply relieved that they had lost nothing more than one boy. Occasionally their thoughts did turn to the boy but they were soon blotted out as they remembered the crime he had committed, and embroidered details about Teon and his family into the tale to make the story even worse, remembering the utter folly of youth. Something like this could have cost many more their lives, could have cost them the torching of their homes, could have cost them their livelihood. Some remembered the horrors of the massacre eighteen years before. One boy was a small price to pay to prevent a repeat of that.

Bohran, the village elder, was even pleased with his work. He had managed to grovel his village out of the darkest moment it had faced for many years. The status quo had been about to be destroyed and he had saved it. The sacrifice of one boy – and lets face it, a boy who had confessed to the crime – had been worth it to save the village, to save their livelihood, to save what they were. Within the space of a day the village had been facing complete disaster, and in his mind he had saved his village from that disaster. Bohran even began to daydream of what this might mean to him, the congratulations, perhaps even reward from "higher places" for his action in saving the village – at last the opportunities he felt had been denied him over the years, the opportunity to leave this hellhole of a town behind.

Only Hesteon was in tears, inconsolable at having lost his son. Hesteon had been proud of Teon, so he felt his loss even more sharply – not only had Teon been taken away from him, but Teon's honour had gone, his own pride for his son destroyed – even Hesteon believed Teon had committed the murder. He was distraught – his son a murderer, the memory of Janci stained.

For Hesteon there was only despair, numbness. He could never have believed his son could do that, yet Teon had confessed, and he had been angry that they wouldn't get paid, and the money had been found in Teon's room in the attic, and surely Teon must have done it. He had lost the wife he had loved so dearly. Now the son whom he loved, whom he dreamed would have joined the army, who would have done well in the army, in service to his country – he too was gone. For Hesteon, his hopes had been destroyed. His dreams were destroyed. Even his reason for life was destroyed. There was only blackness: blackness today, blackness tomorrow, blackness for ever.

Only one person had any real thoughts other than relief or despair. Gowli was confused. It just didn't make sense. Teon was a good lad. He had collected firewood for her. He had dug her garden. He had been quiet, but he was a good lad and sensitive. To her, a widow, childless, in her early seventies and full of arthritis, Teon had been the one person to show her care and love. Gowli was said to have spark: her eyes danced, her face was normally lively with joy, yet lined with pain from the arthritis. Now however, her brow was a furrowed frown. Hesteon was always busy, but somehow Teon had adopted his elderly neighbour. Since his mother had died Gowli had given him the female support he needed. In return Teon made it so much easier for her to live alone in the village, providing the strength she herself had lost many years before. Gowli was confused. She knew Teon – he couldn't do it. Teon was gentle. Sensitive. Teon cared. There was a strength in Teon that allowed him to care. Teon could not kill.

And yet Teon had confessed.... That night Gowli couldn't sleep. Teon. Gone. Teon a murderer? Teon taken? Yet Teon had been the grandson she had never had, who cared with all his being. It wasn't right....

Gowli could not sleep with her confusion.

At some time in the night Teon's sobs had run their course, to be replaced by numbness and sleep. A sleep that was broken, uneasy, tormented, made more difficult by the arms tied behind his back, the cold and damp of the floor. Through his dreams he could see the dead body on the floor of his house. He could see his father's desperate face in the crowd. He could feel the ropes tightened on his arms. He could hear the horses clattering on the stones seemingly for ever. He could feel the pain in his feet. He could hear Magrell's voice whispering. He finally woke in the morning, the cold seeming to eat right to his bones. Teon's body was wracked with pain. His arms still hurt from being tied behind his back, although in the night one of the guards, or someone, had been in after he had gone to sleep to remove them. He had also removed the tattered shoes from Teon's feet. His bottom hurt where he sat all night. His feet hurt from the constant walking the previous day. His head hurt from tears and the effect of the sun beating down on him the previous day. His throat was dry from thirst. His stomach hurt in hunger.

Teon slowly pulled his senses together. At first he thought he was still at home, but the cold and the pain dispelled that notion. Perhaps camping with friends, but he knew he was alone. After what seemed an age, but was only about 10 minutes, Teon had remembered the horrors of the previous day. He remembered the events that led him to be here, cold, sore, alone.

Teon slowly looked around his cell. It was perhaps ten feet square with stone walls and damp, cold floor. On the opposite side from where he sat was the single heavy wooden door covered with metal studs, almost more solid than the stones themselves. The door had a small circle, perhaps a peephole through which the guards could see him, although Teon couldn't be sure, the hole about five feet off the ground. Teon guessed the hole was probably covered from the other side. There was only one other thing in the cell with Teon – an old rusty bucket that he knew instinctively was there as his toilet. The cell was quite high, perhaps ten feet high he thought and it looked as if the ceiling were made of timber. It was lit by a single glass-less barred window at least two feet above Teon's head, a mere eighteen inches square. There was nothing else.

Teon tried to move and found that despite the pain he could move his arms and his feet. He found that moving them gave him some relief, brought a little life back into his body. He gingerly scrambled onto his hands and knees, then steadied himself on the wall as he struggled to his feet. At first putting his weight on his feet was excruciatingly painful after the battering they had taken the previous day, but slowly he moved around the cell, and as he did the stiffness, the pain, the blinding headache receded until he was left with one overwhelming ache – the ache in his stomach from hunger, and was left with one overwhelming desire – for water. Teon walked numbly and slowly around the cell seven or eight times, then sat down against the wall again, his mind unable to think through the events of the previous day. Only three things were real to Teon – his hunger, his even greater thirst, and the despair that this was not Mayeringham, not home. For Teon, his tears had run dry. Now there was only pain and despair and nothingness.

The same morning, following a sleepless night, Gowli had hobbled in her arthritic gait around to see Hesteon. He obviously hadn't slept either. Hesteon opened the door, saw who it was, then without speaking led Gowli into the kitchen. The kitchen was sparsely furnished with a range, some shelves holding food and cooking pots, a table and two chairs. Hesteon slumped onto one of the chairs. Gowli limped into the kitchen and slowly sat on the other chair across from Hesteon, hoping she was welcome. They sat in silence for several minutes until Hesteon looked up and spoke.

Hesteon only had two words: "My son".

Silence broke in again, as the two sat there. Both seemed lost in their own thoughts, until Gowli broke the silence, speaking hesitantly.

"Do you remember that time when Teon went missing? Last autumn wasn't it? Missing overnight, and we had to organise a search party and Bohran called the village council." Gowli's voice began to get stronger as she continued speaking. "And how we had searched through the village. We searched the old storage sheds by the border up there. And then remember how we searched along by the river, and we still found nothing. And how we went over to the great gorge and scrambled along to that to see if he had fallen in. And still found nothing. And then how we sent out messengers to see if he had been spotted perhaps heading for the city, or even heading in to Bayron?

"What a day that was, what a carry-on." She smiled but without humour. "Then do you remember? He appeared as if nothing had happened, except he was carrying that blackbird with an injured wing. How he couldn't understand the fuss. He hadn't realised it had taken that long to catch the bird to bring it back here to make it better? Do you remember how you kept him in for a week after that, how he fed the bird and looked after it? And do you remember the day the blackbird finally flew off into the trees, then up there over the wood." Gowli pointed through the window of the kitchen to some trees just outside the village. "Do you remember the pure joy on his face as he set that bird free? How he danced here that night because the life had been saved?

"I can't believe the same person did this."

Gowli stopped talking and the silence took over again. For many more minutes they sat there until Gowli got to her feet. Hesteon didn't even hear Gowli leave.

Teon heard the guards talking outside the door of his cell, then heard the heavy lock turning in the door. . Teon guessed it was still fairly early in the morning from the little light coming through the window. He continued to sit where he was as the door slowly slid open. The guards stayed outside the door until they were sure they could see Teon, then one of them brought in a tray.

The other guard held his sword while the first entered fully carrying the tray which he put on the floor near Teon. On the tray was a hunk of bread and cup of water. The guard lifted the bread off the tray and threw it on the floor in contempt for Teon. He put the cup down beside the bread where it had landed. He looked at Teon and gestured to the food, saying nothing. Teon moved towards it on hands and knees from where he sat, but as he reached the bread he saw the guard who had gestured to him swing a leg in his direction, then felt a real crack of pain through his side as the guard's boot caught him in his ribs, a crack that caused him to cry out and roll over. In his agony he heard the guards laugh, then heard the footsteps as they walked out to the corridor. He was dimly aware of the door slamming shut again, of the key turning in the lock.

The guards returned to their seats at the end of the corridor. Hamlan had been very popular in the palace, had been very generous to the guards, and they wanted their chance of revenge on the one who, in cowardice, dared to kill the man with his own sword in his sleep.

Teon lay on the floor for several minutes, then moved again. He found he could move, and guessed they had broken nothing. He reached for the cup and drank some of the water thirstily, then picked up the bread and ate greedily; he drank some more of the water but made sure he left half the cup – he would save the rest for later in the day. At least for a moment one element of his suffering had been taken away. Perhaps better to say his hunger and thirst had been replaced by the pain of the bruise in his side where the kick had landed.

By the end of the day Teon had begun to cough. The cold and the damp had got through to his chest. Following the morning food nothing else had happened to him all that day, and his struggles had been made worse by the boredom of sitting in an empty cell.

In the evening the guards had again brought bread and water, although the earlier kick had satisfied their urge to lash out for the moment. This time they had also left three coarse blankets in the cell, and had even brought a third man – probably another prisoner – to change the bucket, simply taking out the used one and replacing it with another rusty one. Through all of this no-one spoke, no-one even looked in Teon's direction again.

The food and blankets had taken perhaps 5 minutes to bring in, and Teon was again left alone. He knew night was coming on as the light in his cell began to fade. At first he lay on the ground and pulled the blankets over him only to feel the cold rising bitterly from the floor. Within a few minutes he had rolled himself in the blankets and sleep had overtaken him again. Even before the light had disappeared, Teon was fast asleep.

Gowli returned in the late afternoon to Hesteon, and made him eat some bread and drink water, laced with some spirits. Hesteon didn't have the interest to eat the meat she brought with her, or even drink the spirits she brought, but Gowli insisted until he had eaten and drunk.

"You must do something" she demanded again of Hesteon, trying to get through to him. After the food and through the subsequent evening Gowli nagged and nagged but seemed to make no impression on him. "You must do something. He could not have done it". She had said it ten, maybe twenty times and still made no impression on Hesteon.

At last he spoke. "He had the money. He had the chance. He admitted it. He must have done it." He shook his head slowly and sadly.

Gowli was not to be deterred. "I don't care what he admitted he could not have done it".

For an hour Gowli tried to get through to Hesteon, but in his self-pity and despair he not only saw Teon as guilty, his mind made him even worse. He suddenly looked hard at Gowli. "Perhaps he even killed Janci". His head slumped once more and he heard nothing more that Gowli had to say, her protestations all to no avail. The horror of the previous day, his chaotic thoughts took all reasoned thought from Hesteon. Teon shown to be a murderer. A murderer. Hesteon convinced himself that Teon had also taken away the one person he still treasured above all others: the wife who had died so young, for no apparent reason. The events, the spirits he had drunk, the horror, the depression, the guilt: all of these worked together to convince him – this monster who had been his son had killed her as well.

Gowli stomped out of Hesteon's home and down the track to Bohran's. Bohran would understand, or at least the Bohran of old would have understood. She was no longer sure however – the body and mind of Bohran was still there, the spirit of the man had long since died. But she still had to try.

Bohran invited her in and pointed her to a soft chair in his study and offered her a drink. He had great respect for this little but powerful lady struggling with arthritis, who had lived with honour and dignity as a widow in their community for many years – her husband had been killed as a young man fighting in the Fethonite army and Gowli had been on her own for 40 years. It was very difficult for a single woman to live on her own in Mayeringham. It was even harder to live there with honour, yet Gowli had done both.

Bohran listened to her, even to her re-telling the blackbird story. He listened to her telling him what Teon was like. Telling him about Teon's love for beauty, from the blackbird to the peacock butterfly to the glorious sunset. Telling him how Teon had looked after her. For many minutes Gowli poured out to Bohran all she knew of Teon.

It was all to no avail. Gowli was suddenly aware that Bohran was sounding like everyone else in the civil service muttering platitudes in response to what Gowli was saying. "Not my business". "Nothing I can do". "We have done our job of saving our community". It all sounded so cold, so uncaring, yet logically it sounded perfect. Bohran was happy to accept that Teon had done it because that is what a civil servant does. Bohran was happy to accept that he had saved the status quo because that was what he felt was required of him. For Bohran, Teon had saved the village by his actions, and that was good for Bohran the civil servant. Even if he had not committed the murder, and everything suggested he had, Bohran felt Teon had done the honourable thing, and that he, Bohran, in some way had saved the village.

Finally Gowli gave up. After listening to the soothing tones of Bohran for several minutes she jumped to her feet and walked to the door, Bohran still talking "...and we have managed to maintain the continuity of our way of life...". His voice stopped as Gowli pulled the door open

As she reached, then opened, the door Gowli suddenly stopped. She turned and pointed at Bohran. She knew she had to used his name as she spoke. "Bohran, you are a coward". Then Gowli was gone.

Bohran sat staring at the door. Something rose within him and he knew with a flash that she was right. Quickly he suppressed the thought, pushed it back down deeply, and was once again the untouched and untouchable civil servant. He continued to write the report he had started before Gowli had arrived, the report of what had happened that he would have to send to Durringham.

3

For Teon the next few days continued as the previous one. In the morning the guards came in with the bread and water, and even once with a banana. In the evenings they came with more bread and water, but this time also bringing the other prisoner with them to change the bucket. Teon had tried to make contact with the other prisoner, had tried to make eye contact, but the other prisoner barely looked in his direction. The days were spent in boredom, the nights rolled in the blankets, sleeping surprisingly well, despite the cough that had developed while he had been in the cell.

For Teon the bruise on his side still hurt but his feet and arms were almost feeling back to normal. He felt weak but that was from lack of food rather than injuries. Teon's cough had established itself and occasionally racked his body, but was getting no worse – the blankets seemed to give him enough warmth to keep the cough from deepening. Teon was frustrated that he was unable to rid himself of the cough, but for Teon the worst was the utter boredom of this existence.

Mentally Teon remained numb, as if the village had never existed. He thought rarely of the past or the future – all there remained was this cell, the cold, the damp and the cough. When he did think of the past his mind went much further back – to his mother, Janci, to the few short years he had spent at school, sometimes to Gowli, the feisty old neighbour, who was the grandmother he had never had. Sometimes his mind went to the future but he had no sense of the future. No-one had spoken to him, nor said what was to happen to him. Nothing had given him any inkling of what the future might hold. He could not even picture a future except to stay in the cell, coughing.

Magrell himself was well pleased. Hamlan was already dead. His funeral had been held, the body buried with full military honours. No-one asked awkward questions. The first part of his plan was already complete. In the cells below was the weapon for the next part of the plan to which he was just putting the finishing touches. In his safe, hidden from everyone else – he had even installed the safe himself – was the final element he needed, the letter. Magrell had plenty to be pleased about, as he turned to the stairs which led down to the cells. Magrell had eaten his evening meal well, and thought that it was time to put the next part of his plan into practice.

As Magrell approached, the guards stood to attention, and Magrell spoke to them briefly. On his order, they led him along the corridor to the cell. They unlocked the door and he dismissed them, allowing them to return to their game of cards.

Teon was awoken from his numbness by the sound of the lock, then was aware of the door swinging open, and a man standing in the doorway. Teon's heart started pumping – for the first time in days something different was happening. The man was probably in his late twenties. His clothes suggested he was a man of high rank: dressed in leather, the finest leather money could buy. His trousers were dark blue, his tunic dark red. Over his shoulder he had a band – the emblem of the leader of the Bayronite army – a position he had gained from the death of Hamlan. At his side he had a sword in an ornately decorated scabbard. However, Teon noticed little of this. All that struck him was the bright light reflecting from the diamonds of the hilt of the sword.

Teon felt he recognised the man, but wasn't sure from where until he spoke. Then the events in the village leapt back to his mind as he recognised the man who had found the body, who demanded the culprit, who accused Hesteon, who led Teon tied beside his horse, who finally had led Teon to this cell.

Magrell slowly entered the cell, then sat on his haunches in front of Teon who was sat slumped against the wall. He knew the boy was no match for him and would not make any attempt to attack him, particularly since the cough had taken over his chest.

Very slowly Magrell adjusted how he sat, then even more slowly looked at Teon. Teon felt his eyes held by the man he knew was called Magrell.

Magrell leant forward and whispered very quietly to Teon. "Tomorrow, boy, you will be executed".

As soon as the words had been said ice gripped Teon's heart, the ice of fear. For days his feelings had seemed to die, but suddenly they were very alive and gripping him hard in the stomach. Not once did he think to doubt what Magrell had said to him.

"At dawn, you will be taken from here and you will hang." Magrell continued. "To think, you did nothing wrong, and you will be hanged for it. It is a horrific death, so I am told." Magrell gave Teon an ironic smile.

Suddenly everything came flooding back to Teon. He HAD done nothing wrong. The events of that day scrambled through his mind, his memory, his heart. It was so unfair – he had done nothing wrong, and he was to die. He didn't want to die. He didn't want to end here. He had not had life. He had not joined the army. It was all wrong. It was all so unfair.

Teon tried to scream but no sound came out of his sick chest. He tried to speak but Magrell raised his hand. Magrell continued speaking. "Wouldn't you love to be somewhere else? Back home. Back in Fethon. Back with your family, your friends?" All the memories of childhood flooded back to Teon in the instant. "Wouldn't you just love to run away? Wouldn't you just like to walk out of here, escape?"

Magrell stood to his feet. "Tomorrow you will hang until you die. It is a slow and painful way to go". He turned and left. Teon heard the doors slam, heard Magrell's feet disappearing along the corridor. He heard the laughter of the guards as Magrell must have made a joke. But something was not right. Teon's mind whirled – there was something not right....

It must have been the early hours of the morning when Teon jolted awake. Remarkably, after Magrell had left, and in spite of Magrell's threat, he dropped off to sleep, but suddenly in the early hours of the morning that had all changed and he was wide awake. It struck him what was wrong. Magrell had shut the door and left. But the key had not been turned in the lock. Magrell hadn't locked it. The guards hadn't come to relock the door. Teon knew well the clanking sound of the door being locked, and he hadn't heard it. Instantly Teon had his plan. It was a plan based on, and driven by, the fear and panic for the events of the next morning. He had a single plan – flight. If he could get out of the cell – and Magrell had forgotten to lock it – he could find some-where to hide until daylight, then could run out of the palace and the city gate and hope.... It was his only hope.

Teon moved over to the door but there was no handle. He looked at the door then put his finger to the eye-hole. He jammed his finger into the eye-hole. He pulled, praying that the door would not squeak. Nothing happened. He pulled again. Very slowly and silently the door began to move, very slowly the door began to swing open. Teon's heart was beating fast.

Teon let go of the eye-hole as the door moved with its own momentum, then when the door was eighteen inches ajar he looked out into the corridor. Darkness. There was a light at the end of the corridor, but no shape of a person. Even the guards were gone. Teon went into the corridor, then slowly headed towards the only light he could see: the light was a candle on the wall facing the corridor along which Teon was slowly making his way. Teon came to the end of the corridor, where it joined a larger corridor. To the left he could hear voices, men laughing, talking – perhaps the guard room. Teon immediately turned right, following the corridor away from the men's voices. For some time he walked carefully and silently along the corridor that was lit by candles on holders in the wall. He turned a corner and saw a flight of steps going upwards. He hesitated, then began to climb the steps, suddenly aware of how weak he had become in the cell with only minimal food.

Halfway up the stairs Teon stopped to rest, but within moments was at the top. The steps had led onto a landing with three other corridors off. Teon had no idea which way to go. The ones to the left and to the right were well lit, the one ahead, through a small door, dark and much smaller.

Suddenly he heard voices – perhaps two men were approaching from the left corridor. At the same time he heard footsteps approaching from the right. There was only one thing he could do: Teon quickly moved into the dark corridor oppo-site, his only hope of not being seen. He stood as still as possible, praying his cough would not give him away. The voices approached – Teon held his breath, then the two men from the left appeared in the light on the landing, and were joined by the man from the right. Teon could see that they were guards. From the dark shadows barely eight feet away Teon could watch them but couldn't be seen. They stopped on the landing, talking to each other. Teon could even make out what they were talking about: the quiet, nothing happening, breakfast coming up. With his heart beating, Teon desperately hoped they would not come down his corridor. Desperately he hoped he would not start coughing.

The three men must have talked on the landing for three or four minutes, then slowly entered the corridor to the right that was well lit. Teon missed one of them glancing down his corridor, smiling to the others before the three men left together. Teon breathed a sigh of relief. He wanted away from the landing as quickly as possible but felt the well-lit corridor was too dangerous. He continued away from the landing, heading along the darkened corridor where he had been hiding.

The corridor seemed to go on for ages. It was very narrow but generally too high for Teon to make out the ceiling. At times there were pools of water on the floor. Sometimes Teon found himself climbing stairs, other times going down stairs. At regular intervals Teon stopped to catch his breath – he found the simple effort of walking exhausting. Climbing stairs was even worse. Overall he felt he was going up rather than down. Once he had seen a light on the floor, but as he approached found it was a hole into a corridor which was well lit, the floor of the corridor ten feet below. The light also showed him that his corridor continued ahead into the dark.

At first the corridor didn't strike Teon as strange – he had just been pleased to get away from the landing and the guards. However, with time it seemed incredibly long with no doors, apart from the one hole into the corridor below. Very occasionally there had been a candle that had kept him going away from his cell. He had been walking slowly along the corridor for fear of making a noise and had rested regularly, guessing that he may have been in the corridor for fifteen or twenty minutes. Where could a corridor like this go? What could it be for?

Teon came upon the corner suddenly in a particularly dark stretch of the corridor – the corridor turned at right angles very suddenly. Ahead was an open door, with a dull glow the other side – a bit like a room with moonlight shining in to it. Teon felt this might be the beginning of the time to look for somewhere to hide until daytime, to look for a way out of the castle.

Teon edged forward very slowly until he had reached the door, then looked into the room. The room was totally silent and was, as he had guessed, lit by moonlight. In his curiosity about the room he missed the light cotton tripwire across the corridor that his leg broke when he turned the corner. He wasn't aware of the alarm he had set off a couple of rooms away.

In the room Teon could make out a four-poster bed, some pieces of furniture, a couple of doors – all became clear as his eyes adjusted to the moonlight. Slowly Teon edged into the room and moved to the first door. He put his ear to the door but could hear nothing. He tried the door, but it was clearly locked, with no key on Teon's side.

Teon moved to the other door and again put his ear to it listening. Again there was no sound. Teon tried the handle and felt it turn easily in his hand.

Suddenly the handled was turning more quickly than he was turning it.

Suddenly he felt the door begin to open towards him.

CRASH. The door was thrown violently open. Teon was thrown onto his back. Suddenly the room was flooded with light. Within moments the room was full of soldiers and others milling around. He heard a voice shout: "LOOK".

Teon could make out that everyone was looking towards the bed, except for one who had thrown something damp and wet – perhaps a glass of water – onto Teon. In the bed lay the Emperor, eyes staring emptily into space. He was pinned to the bed by a sword thrust through his chest, blood covering his chest, spreading to the floor.

Slowly soldiers looked around to Teon – he lay on the floor gasping for breath after being winded by the blow of the door. Teon's clothes were covered with blood.

4

The small woman sat on the bench looking around her. In Gresk she was called Hansa. She looked at the work that had taken her fourteen years to achieve, realising how little it seemed. Two larger rectangular ramshackle wooden buildings joined by a corridor perhaps ten yards long. Off the corridor was two doors, one leading to toilets, the other to the storeroom – separate shacks built on the side of the corridor. It wasn't just the two buildings that were built of timber – the whole thing was. Each of the two bigger buildings would take a dozen beds, with little space for anything else. Cooking and food preparation was done in the open; in wet weather under a canopy at the front of the main door off the long corridor.

Hansa listened to the sounds of work and chatter around the buildings: twelve others had joined her – some widows, others servants no longer required by masters, two of them Bayronites who had joined her group voluntarily. Between them they did everything. They had built the commune. They cared for the sick who came their way. They tended the gardens to give themselves food. They walked the streets of Gresk looking for people who needed their help. Three times now she had simply sat in the cold with beggars as their lives came to an end, too frail to even bring to the commune. There was so little to show for fourteen years.

It was all so different from the great dreams many years before. Then she had lived far away to the North in the great wilderness with her clan, living the nomadic life of the North people. Fourteen years before they had camped in their winter grazing grounds and gathered, as they did each evening after eating, around the great fire.

The evening was so startling that Hansa could picture it as if it had happened only a minute before. The fire burning, a great flame leaping high, the flame turning into a figure, leaping across

27

the space to her. And then gone. Left in Hansa was the feeling she had to go south. She had to build bridges. She had to make contact with the southern peoples. She had to bring them back to the fire.

She left the next day with the blessing of her clan, and took four days to reach Gresk. She had arrived and set up home on waste ground – at first building a shelter with a few branches and mud – and began to help her neighbours. With time she had learnt to speak as a resident of Gresk, she built a larger home and developed the gardens. In time, on the force of her personality, the commune had slowly grown to what it had become today. In those years she had learnt to speak as a southerner as well – for her that had been the simple part.

Through all the previous fourteen years Hansa had a feeling of disappointment. She had seen the face in the flames many times, but her great dreams seemed to have come to very little – a group of twelve women used by some, respected by others, scorned by many. For fourteen years work there was so little to show in bringing the peoples together.

Until now. The feeling of disappointment was gone. Hansa didn't even know why. The face had not said anything to her. The city of Gresk was in mourning for the murdered Emperor. Everything pointed to a time of gloom and depression. Yet there was something that was saying to her – now is the time. Now is the real beginning.

Hansa sat alone on the bench until late in the evening. She rose, excitement beginning to course through her veins. This WAS the beginning....The beginning of what?

Nothing escaped the grapevine. Within a couple of days the whole village of Mayeringham heard what had happened to the Emperor, and that a young Fethonite boy had done it. At first the name didn't arrive with the rumours but everyone in Mayeringham knew it was Teon. Behind the backs of Gowli, Hesteon and Bohran they gossiped of nothing else. No-one needed to say anything to Hesteon – within a further twenty-four hours travellers were openly using the name "Teon" as the guilty one, so that Hesteon didn't need to hear from his own villagers.

Hesteon was distraught. How could his son have done this? Killing Hamlan had been awful but the village had escaped; Mayeringham had been saved. This was so much worse. This could lead to war. If they could find something to link Teon with the Fethonite army or the Fethonite royal family it would give the Bayronites the excuse they needed to invade. They might not even need an excuse – perhaps it would be enough that a Fethonite had murdered the Emperor, or maybe they could manufacture some evidence themselves. The slaughter would begin at Mayeringham, and Fethon had no hope against the might of the Bayronite army. Perhaps they were preparing to invade already, perhaps only held back by the mourning of the nation for their Emperor who had been highly respected by his people.

Not only Hesteon saw this, Bohran too was in his office mulling over in his mind the events of a week ago, and the stories that were coming out of Bayron now. He also heard the words of Gowli: "Bohran, you are a coward", ringing in his head. Perhaps if he had acted differently when the first murder happened in their village instead of taking the easy way out none of this would have happened, the threat hanging over the village and the nation would not be there. Was he responsible for what was happening? Could he have done anything differently? A corner of his mind told him that he had done it wrongly, he should have sent word to Durringham concerning what had happened, but he had simply grasped the easiest answer. For Bohran there was a foreboding gloom: that all his smugness at his apparent success had been totally misplaced – things were suddenly far far worse than when Hamlan had been killed. The easy way out proved to be an awful trap for his whole country.

Overnight the village had been converted from a busy place, doing business, working hard, to a village hanging on every word of gossip. Teon was talked about. Hesteon was discussed, but avoided by everyone. The possibility of war was on everyone's lips. The future looked dark for everyone. Somehow work lost all importance as the darkness loomed. Some simply drank. Others began to pack. Everyone waited on every rumour, questioned every person who passed through the village, who came over the border, although they knew the number of travellers had reduced considerably. Everyone had a growing feeling that this could be the end for their village, a feeling made all the greater as rumours gathered pace.

Only one person – Gowli – remained certain Teon was innocent. It was that blackbird. But Gowli knew – there was nothing she, crippled by arthritis, could do. She knew no-one would listen to an old woman whose only evidence was a black-bird. She too could see that darkness was rolling in over the village and nation.

In Durringham, the capital of Fethon, Jayron was also worried. Jayron may have been a King of peace, but he was also a person who made sure he knew what was happening. He had heard of Hamlan's death, and the boy taken off to Bayron. His advisors had told him the content of Bohran's report. With the death of the Emperor he also knew the boy's name: Teon. The name meant nothing to him.

Over the next two or three days Jayron was in conference with his advisors. He too was aware of the seriousness of the situation. He had met the Bayronites's and was under no doubt they would link this murder to the rulers of Fethon. Jayron was under no doubt that his country was under the severest threat it had ever known. He was certain that the only reason for delay was to sort out the succession in Bayron. The Emperor had only one son and no daughters. The son – Hamlan – had been killed only a few weeks before. Jayron knew he had to act if there was to be any possibility of staving off war, invasion and inevitable defeat. He eventually announced his decision: "I will go to the funeral". He would travel, with a small group, to Bayron to take part in the Emperor's funeral. As soon as he had made his decision he sent messengers to Gresk to say he would be coming.

It was the only answer. Perhaps he could show they were not involved by being present at the funeral. Perhaps he could nego-tiate a way to bring peace. If that failed perhaps he could offer himself in some way to save his people. The last thing Jayron wanted was bloodshed, massacres in his nation. He desperately hoped he would get the chance to speak.

Jayron prepared for the journey, and decided to take only 8 soldiers with him as a guard. Each soldier would have a pack horse for supplies and gifts, for the accoutrements of a royal visit. Jayron set out in the early morning for the journey to Gresk, the capital of Bayron.

It was the early hours of the morning – there were only a small group of customers left in the Lion Tavern, built into the city walls on the north side of Gresk. The Lion had always been part of Gresk. It was the one place in the whole country where you would see royalty and commoners mixing together, united in the desire for an alcoholic stupor.

The landlord had thrown all the other customers out hours before, but he dare not throw these out. He continued to serve the ale they demanded. The small group arrived late in the evening, and into the early hours they became progressively louder as both men and women in the group drank more and more.

"We drink to the beginning of a new era". One stood to his feet and was talking in a slurred voice. He steadied himself on the table. "We drink to the beginning of a new reign". The man had the apparent rapt attention of his companions as he drank from a tankard, slopping half of the ale down his tunic. Again he held onto the table and continued in the drunken voice. "Friends, tonight cousin Emperor Pellaig was found dead. Cousin Pellaig got all he deserved. Friends, we drink to a new Emperor..." He paused dramatically, "...me".

The man who was speaking when sober stood about six feet tall, with good looks that other men dreamt of. He was in his late thirties, and was rarely seen without a beautiful girl on his arm. His clothes were of the best quality, the most fashionable colour and style: dashing, except at times like this – times when he drank too much and the spilt drink stained whatever he was wearing. His nose had just a hint of red, a sign of too much drink sustained over too many years.

His friends looked quizzically to each other. After drinking from the tankard he continued in his drunken slur. "No other relatives – I'm the cousin, I'm the closest," he said in a conspiratorial voice. Then in a louder voice he continued. "And friends, we drink to an even better future. More parties. More women. More drink." Again a pause. Then his voice rose higher and louder. "When I'm Emperor we'll have all we want, and no-one will stop us". His friends roared their drunken agreement. All drank their tankards dry then demanded more drink. The landlord filled each of their tankards to the rim.

The "new Emperor" slumped into his seat, then pulled himself upright, and pointed at his friends. There was suddenly an anger in his voice. "Do you know what I want most?" His friends became silent again. "I'm going to have that cold-hearted bitch sharing my bed."

The man was stirring his anger. He began to rant: "When her husband was on the eastern campaign she was happy enough to come to my arms. Five months without cousin Pellaig and she wanted me then. But cousin Pellaig comes back and I'm dirt again. Dirt ever since. Muck on her boot – that's how she looks at me. Treats me. Well, I tell you this – when I'm Emperor she'll be the tart in my bed. She'll have no choice but to be my bride. Stuck up bitch. I'll make her the laughing stock she deserves to be, I will make her suffer for what she has done to me." The man ran out of steam, his tirade coming to a halt.

Twenty minutes later the men and women staggered into the palace and slumped into a drunken sleep in the great dining hall, in front of the fire – they had gone there in search of more ale but had found none.

Rumours of Jayron's visit to Gresk quickly spread through both Bayron and Fethon. The villagers of Mayeringham knew of the visit the evening before Jayron set out. They were also nervous: they knew that the king would stop there and would probably talk to Bohran. The king would ask some awkward questions. The villagers were not surprised when Jayron and his guards rode in about midday asking for refreshment. The guards remained outside in the village square with their horses. The villagers were too reticent to come and speak to them once they had provided the refreshment they needed.

Bohran himself met the king and greeted him. He took him into his home for lunch and drink. Bohran produced the best food he could find, and over lunch told the king about Teon. Bohran told him about Hesteon and the events surrounding Hamlan's death. He told how the boy had confessed, and had been taken prisoner by the Bayronites. Jayron frowned hard at this – he did not like a single one of his citizens handed over to another nation whatever had happened. He frowned but said nothing – he hadn't the time, and that could be sorted out later. Bohran also spoke of their fears, of the rumours they had heard of war and invasions, but Jayron himself had already heard these and wanted to return to the facts. There was little more that Bohran could add. Bohran was puzzled – he explained to the king how he had saved the village from destruction, expecting Jayron to congratulate him in some way. Jayron replied icily: "The destruction of one young person is just as bad".

Jayron also summoned Hesteon, but his encounter with Hesteon told him nothing new – he was a man in despair, so much in despair that he could barely speak except in monosyllables, and certainly had no spirit to defend his son. After a few minutes Jayron dismissed Hesteon, knowing at this moment there was nothing he could do for this man in his suffering.

Jayron finished his food and rose to his feet, thanked his host for the meal and put a bag of coins on the table. Bohran knew this was the king's habit, and that the coins would more than cover anything he spent. Despite the generous payment Bohran also knew that somehow he had angered the king.

Jayron went outside, walked across the square, took his horse from one of his guards and began to mount. Just then he heard a woman shout out. He saw her limping in a rush across the square in front of Bohran's house as fast as she could. Jayron waited and watched the old lady hobble towards him. When she reached Jayron she grabbed his left leg, shouting out – "he didn't do it, he didn't do it". Two of the guards quickly dismounted and tried to pull Gowli from the king, but she was not to be moved.

Gowli continue to shout: "Teon is innocent. He didn't do it".

After a few moments of undignified struggle the king said one word: "Enough". It was sufficient to stop both the guards and Gowli immediately. Gowli released his leg and was dragged by the guards away from Jayron. The king dismounted from his horse and looked Gowli straight in the eye. To Gowli it felt like his eyes peered straight into her very being. Jayron gestured to the guards to release her, then spoke in a quiet but commanding voice that was not to be disobeyed. "Speak, woman".

Gowli quickly spoke. "Teon's a good lad. He was my neighbour, like a grandson to me. He couldn't have done it. He wasn't like that. The boy loved beauty. Looked after me. Helped his father. A good boy". The words gabbled out on top of each other. Jayron's eyes never left Gowli, but he gently lifted a hand to silence her. For long long moments Jayron held her gaze. Gowli felt she could hide nothing from this man and the piercing compassionate stare.

Jayron again spoke tersely. "Thank you". With that he was on his horse, he and his guards were gone.

Jayron and the guards rode at a trot into Bayron. They rode silently, only accompanied by the sounds of horses hooves on cobbles, riding through villages on their way to the capital. In many cases they were ignored, in others there was clear hostility towards the Fethonite party when people recognised them or guessed who they were. Every now and then they were jeered; sometimes a stone was thrown at them. Jayron also kept his eyes open and noticed the signs that some sort of military preparations were being made. In one village a number of horses had been gathered together. In another village too many men were carrying weapons. In yet another village extra tents and men were standing in groups with nothing obvious to do. All the signs of a national muster beginning, of a country just being mobilised for war. On the road itself Jayron's group regularly met small groups of men riding, again with all the look of military messengers carrying orders around the countryside.

Jayron rode on apparently confidently, but inside he was turning over and over what might happen, the decisions he had made. He hadn't mustered his army. He hadn't called up the reserve. He hadn't even deployed the standing army for defence. He still believed there was a chance for peace, but was he simply being naive? He still believed he could save the country by talking, and he had put his money where his mouth was by not building his defences. If he could do it by talking, then he did not need to deploy the army. But was that a foolish choice? Jayron was more uncertain of himself now than he had ever been. His one great skill in these circumstances – he could hide that uncertainty better than any man he knew – he continued to ride boldly and confidently.

Only one thing had really upset Jayron – the woman in the village. Until he had met her he had accepted the boy's confession. He had not even planned to see the boy when he went to the Bayronite capital. The boy would simply take the punishment due for his crime, however brutally that was applied by the Bayronites. Now that was all different. He already knew the boy's name – Teon. Now he knew he was innocent – somewhere within he knew the old woman was right. Jayron knew there was the easy option, that he could still let the boy be punished and perhaps save the nation, avert the war. But he wasn't just a boy, he was a citizen, a person with a name, he was called Teon. For Jayron, refuse true justice to one person and your own honour is destroyed. Refuse justice to one person and your whole nation is sullied.

Late in the afternoon Jayron and his party found themselves approaching the western gateway of Gresk. Gresk was a huge city compared to Durringham. The walls seemed to rise higher and higher: an illusion made all the greater as the Western gate of Gresk was at the top of a long hill. The illusion of size was emphasised even further by the towers of the great palace reaching to the sky, the palace itself rising above the city walls. The Emperor's palace stood to the east of the city square and was built on a man-made mound, made to act as a keep for the city should the city walls ever yield in battle. The city walls never had yielded. The great city walls, perhaps twenty feet high and heavily defended, surrounded the main part of the city, but Gresk had grown, and had outgrown its walls. All around the city were small groups of huts, shanty settlements and markets. The residents of those areas were happy to make their living in the big city even though they could not find homes there, ready to run inside the city walls at first sign of trouble.

Jayron and his party were met at the palace gate by Magrell and a small group of army officers. Jayron was greeted formally but with no warmth. He and his guards were shown to quarters which were best described as spartan. Magrell curtly informed them that the funeral rites would begin at nine, four days hence, and left. It was the welcome that Jayron had expected.

5

After Teon was knocked to the ground by the door flying open, the next few minutes were confused. There were all the soldiers rushing in to the room. Shouts of "He's dead, the Emperor is dead" rang in his ears. There were people crying, shouting, pushing. Suddenly there was a crowd looking at him, and he became aware that he felt wet all over. He briefly noticed that what made him wet was bright red. He felt someone catch hold of his hair and pull him hard to his feet. Teon cried out in pain, but was cut short by a hard blow to his face. This was rapidly followed by his head being pushed to the other side, a blow to the other side of his face. In the pain his ears were ringing and his legs buckled, but he was held upright this time by his arms. Finally Teon screamed and bent double as he felt a punch to his stomach, winding him further and leaving him with little strength, gasping desperately for breath. In the daze of the pain, the events, he was quickly hauled back down corridors, past rooms, past screaming faces. Within minutes he was back in front of the cell from which he had come.

The guards who dragged him there opened the door, dragged him into the cell and threw him brutally against the wall opposite the door. Teon was winded of the little breath he had recovered from the earlier punch to his stomach. The guards stepped back and watched as he slid down the wall, landing on the floor and toppling to his side. Teon gasped for breath, blood coming from a cut on his chin where his head had hit the wall. One of the guards lashed out with a final kick that caught Teon harshly on the arm. The guards sneered, then left.

For many minutes Teon lay on the floor trying to recover his breath, gasping. Part of him wanted to scream with the pain, but he had no breath to make the scream happen. His mind told him that he had escaped. He had been free. He knew it had all gone horribly wrong. He was aware his top was all wet and red. He could feel that blood was trickling from his own mouth and from the graze on his chin. He vaguely knew, just, that they had found him killing the Emperor. Now he was back in his cell and hurting, hurting far more than before.

Finally after perhaps twenty minutes Teon felt he could move. His gasping had eased, and he tried to scramble to sitting. As he moved he screamed out from the pain that shot through his arm. He looked at his arm and saw that it was sticking out in an odd direction. Teon realised that the final kick had broken his left arm just below the elbow. Teon was certain – this was the end of his life, he would never get through this alive. In his thoughts and in his pain Teon passed out of consciousness – the only escape from his suffering and the horrors surrounding him.

Magrell lay back on the couch in his quarters – four rooms, sumptuously decorated on the north side of the palace. Eight hours before the Emperor had been found apparently killed by the boy who had escaped from his cell. It was easy to show that he had entered the secret escape tunnel from the Emperor's bedroom and taken himself in the Emperor's quarters where the Emperor slept. Everyone believed that Teon had killed the Emperor with his own sword, apparently in the same way as he had killed Hamran only days before. It had taken little organisation to guide the boy along the corridor to the Emperors bedroom, and to make sure someone threw a glass of blood over him. No-one was in any doubt – this alien boy in his anger and thirst for revenge had taken the opportunity, when it had presented itself, to kill the Emperor.

Magrell allowed a smile to pass over his lips. The plan was going well, much better than he thought it could, thanks to the boy. With the boy's involvement it allowed him to expand his plan further, allowed his ambition even fuller reign. His original plan was simply to take the place of the Emperor – this boy gave him the opportunity to expand his empire beyond the boundaries of his own country. Magrell had killed the heir to the throne, the only son of the Emperor. He had killed the Emperor himself. In both cases not one person suspected that he had done it. There was the boy, and even if there hadn't been, everyone knew that Magrell was the loyal leader of the Bayronite army who had reached the top as a commoner. He was a person who had no opportunity to get any higher – he was not of the royal family, he was not connected to the royal family. He could never be Emperor. But that was about to change.

There was a knock on the door. Magrell stood to his feet, went to the door and opened it. At the door stood a woman, dressed simply in a white gown, her black hair tied in a knot on her head. Haren was the wife of Pellaig, the former Emperor. She was a tall slender woman who brought a true sense of dignity to her role as Emperor's wife. She was called mother of the nation, and was highly respected by the people. Although respected she was difficult to love because she brought tremendous inner strength to her role and was never seen as vulnerable, her mask never wavering. Few knew the real person, the loneliness, the fears that Haren carried behind that mask. Haren, however, knew her role: she didn't need the love of the people, their respect gave her all the status she needed.

"Come in". Magrell welcomed Haren to his quarters, and showed her to a cushioned seat opposite his. Magrell could see no tears on Haren's face – he knew she would never let anyone see the tears she might shed in her sadness – and tears she would shed because she truly loved the Emperor: the tears would only be shed in private.

"I have invited you here, my Lady", continued Magrell, after he had ensured Haren was comfortably seated, "to offer my deepest sympathy on the tragic death of your husband". Haren nodded her head in thanks. "To say how much he will be missed by all of us". Magrell continued with a few more of the typical platitudes all people make in this sort of situation.

"Of course", said Magrell, "if there is anything I can do for you through this hard time then you must let me know." The Empress genuinely seemed to appreciate Magrell's concern as well as respecting Magrell for his strength and loyalty to her husband and the armed forces.

"However," continued Magrell after a pause, "There is an issue of immediate concern we need to sort out – the succession".

Haren was awoken out of her own thoughts, suddenly aware that there was a different agenda here than she had suspected.

She knew Magrell had invited her so he could offer his commiseration, and perhaps loyalty as the leader of the army; she did not think he would have any other role to play in the events surrounding the death. Why was he talking of the succession?

After a pause to allow the Empress to switch her mind to the new subject, Magrell pressed on. "The situation, as you are aware, your majesty, is extremely difficult. The Emperor has no direct heir – Hamlan, sadly, is no longer with us. You yourself cannot reign because a woman cannot reign in our land. In this situation the Emperor's nearest male relative becomes Emperor."

Magrell paused before continuing. "Would you want him to be Emperor?"

Haren's mind had fully switched on to what Magrell was saying. She certainly did not want Ganerr to be Emperor. Her husband's cousin, a drinker, womaniser, and worst of all for the nation which he would rape for his own ends, greedy – he should never be Emperor. Magrell looked closely into Haren's face, aware that as well as her loathing for Ganerr there was something else in her bearing. Haren was remembering the stupid and brief affair she had with Ganerr many years before when her husband was away for many months in the East, in the days when she had been young and naive. It had only lasted a few weeks and Haren always avoided Ganerr as much as she could but the memory left her feeling stained. Unclean. Haren was a very different person now, but the memories still made her feel shame. Fortunately for Haren, Ganerr had been very careful never to refer to it outside a close circle of friends – to be known as the person who seduced the Emporer's wife would certainly have led to his own death.

Magrell continued, again after a pause. "There is, of course, your majesty, an alternative. Ganerr is loathed as much by the council, by the people and by the army as he is by you. They do not want him as Emperor any more than you do." Haren was now giving Magrell complete attention – there was something here that she had not been expecting.

Magrell was still speaking. "There is, of course, an alternative. If you were to stand before the council and declare that you would marry the right person to be Emperor, that you would marry the right person so that you could reign from, as it were, the back seat, and if that person was respected, the council would accept the marriage and accept that person to be Emperor in order to keep Ganerr out."

For many moments Magrell watched Haren as she thought silently about what Magrell had said.

Magrell knew Haren was an astute lady, and there was only one answer she could give. "Who do you think that should be?"

Magrell again paused before he replied. "Me".

"I don't think that..." Haren had started, but stopped when Magrell held up his hand. He knew she would not accept marriage to him, a commoner who had simply made it to the top in the army. But Magrell had a trump card.

"Your majesty, I think I have another matter you should consider before you make your decision".

Magrell stood to his feet ignoring Haren, then walked over to a door and disappeared into another room to the safe he had there. Two or three minutes later he returned with a piece of paper in his hand, and sat back in his chair.

"Your majesty, can I read you this letter?"

Magrell opened the piece of paper slowly for effect. He glanced at Haren, then began to read. "My dearest Ganerr, I miss you so much. If only I could come and be with you, if only I could say goodbye to that wretched man. My dear Ganerr, I adore you and love you with all my being...." As Magrell continued to read, Haren went deathly pale, the assured and dignified exterior rapidly collapsing. Magrell watched Haren in amusement, an amusement he did not show on his face. There were two more pages which Magrell insisted on reading in full, pages that became more and more graphic in description.

Magrell lowered the letter to his lap. "I think, your majesty, that you will know the signature at the end of the letter". Magrell spoke calmly, but underneath knew he was triumphant. When the letter had fallen into his hands – he was lucky to have a spy at Ganerr's house who read, or tried to read all the letters Ganerr received – he knew he had won the jackpot. He knew this letter could be his passport to position, to the very top. He knew this letter was more valuable than gold to the ambition he kept hidden so well.

He knew also that if he married Haren, he would never give her the chance to "reign from the back seat."

Haren remained silent for several minutes, her mind whirling. How had he obtained this letter that she had sent to Ganerr? Her affair with Ganerr was over, had only lasted a few weeks, had taken place many years ago. Then, as much as she loathed Ganerr, she had also been physically attracted to him and their affair had been physical and torrid.

It was Magrell who broke the silence. "I think, Your majesty, that this letter could cause you tremendous embarrassment. The conclusion people may come to, perhaps, is that you and Ganerr hired a foreign assassin to kill your son and husband....I think, your majesty, that this could be very bad for you." Magrell was enjoying his power over Haren and pushed it further for his own enjoyment, as much as he knew he had already won the encounter. "I would presume that the funeral for an executed Emperor's wife would not be as grand an affair as her husband's funeral...." He paused again, watching the Empress squirm, before continuing. "This might also lead to civil war as we try to fix a successor. On the other hand the letter could return to my safe and we could simply get married...."

Again, the silence descended on the room, Magrell sitting comfortably, confident in his triumph, the Empress a pale shadow of the woman who had entered the room barely twenty minutes before. At last the Empress answered, defeated, her voice barely a whisper. "We will get married."

Teon remained unconscious for perhaps 8 hours – a mixture of shock, pain and tiredness, but over the next few days life returned to the sort of routine it had before the death of the Emperor, although with his injuries the routine was much harsher on Teon. Food was brought to him twice a day. The other prisoner changed his bucket every night. The prisoner had also been allow to strap splints around the arm that had been broken, but the whole process had been excruciatingly painful. There were no anaes-thetics, nothing to dull the pain as the prisoner tied the bandages around the sticks that he used. Teon had to be held down by the guards as the bandages were tied and his cries pierced the cell block. Teon had also been given a new rough shirt to wear – the one covered with blood had been replaced. This was replaced at the same time as the splints had been fixed to his arm.

Teon's overall health was also affected by the treatment he received. He still had the cough, but it was now much harsher. The bruising on his face had come out, and he was now blue and yellow on one side of his head. The punch in the stomach had also taken much of his energy, and although his breathing was not painful unless he yawned, it was uncomfortable. Teon could not see how much thinner he had become either, how much paler, how much his hair had become lank, how much of a wispy beard he had grown. For Teon, now, there was only the cell, the bread and water, the cold and damp. Life had long since departed – now there was only existence.

Two days later Haren, the Empress, had declared that she intended to marry Magrell. It was necessary to make the marriage before the council met to appoint the successor to Pellaig. The following day the marriage ceremony took place – a quiet private affair suitable at a time of mourning, and that same day Magrell was declared Emperor. Many of the council were unhappy with Magrell as a common man who had worked his way to the top of the army, but most were aware that the alternatives would be much worse. Few could see Ganerr as leader. Many held grudges against him, often for what he had done to wives and daughters, others jealous of him and his good looks. Many saw that there would be civil war ahead if there was no clear leader. Even so a few voted against, but they were a small minority. Magrell was Emperor, Emperor of the Bayronite nation. Now there was just the final part of his plan, and that would take place at the funeral....

6

"We have got to go to the funeral". Gowli was yet again at Hesteon's House, her face inches from Hesteon's face. "We have got to go and see your son".

Hesteon was a pale shadow of the man he had been. The man whom a few weeks before had stood muscular and proud had become stooped and round shouldered. Since his son had been taken away he had sunk into a despair. He could barely even remember meeting the king. Even the home he kept as a tribute to his wife Janci had not been tended. In the room where Hamlan had been murdered there were still bloodstains on some of the furniture and soaked into the floor. Hesteon wasn't eating as well as he should. He was drinking too much alcohol. He did nothing around the house apart from making the odd loaf of bread for food. In the two weeks since that awful day Hesteon had changed. Before he had been a proud, fit man in his early forties. Now he had seemingly shrunk. His back was bent. He was nothing of the man he had been. And every day Gowli went to him he looked worse.

Gowli insisted again: "We must go – it is our only chance to see your son".

On the day that Gowli had grabbed Jayron's leg and had spoken to him, Hesteon had been horrified – you don't do that to kings. Yet nothing would stop Gowli. "We have to go and see him. We have to go and find out." Each time Hesteon either shook his head, or continue staring into space.

At last Gowli had snapped. "Hesteon – you are a bigger coward than Bohran. He is frightened for the village. You – you're scared of nothing but the truth. Bohran may be a coward but you are ten times worse. This is your son." Somehow it roused Hesteon out of his despair, roused him to anger.

He shouted at Gowli. "I am not a coward".

Gowli replied quietly. "If you are not a coward then go to Gresk".

They looked a strange couple as they left early the next morning. Gowli, dressed in a hessian cloak tied tightly at her neck, covering her long black rough dress, riding on the donkey. As well as Gowli, the donkey carried their provisions, tied in a sack behind the saddle. Gowli's arthritis would not allow her to walk more than a few hundred yards. Hesteon walked grumpily beside her, saying little as he trudged along the rocky track into Bayron, the path his son had taken barely two weeks before.

Occasionally Gowli walked a short way herself "to keep her joints moving" but most of the time Gowli rode and Hesteon walked. At mid morning they stopped to drink water from a stream across their path; at midday they stopped to eat the bread they brought with them. Otherwise their journey was uneventful until well into the late afternoon – they were an insignificant couple ignored by most, hardly even noticed as they trudged through the Bayronite villages on the road to Gresk.

The path led them through fields, grasslands, occasionally through woodland or through a village. Late in the day they came to a place where the path entered a shallow dry valley. As the valley narrowed, the path became rockier and began to rise. As they climbed, the path entered a narrow gully.

In the narrow dry ravine they were suddenly aware of odd noises ahead of them. They could see nothing – there was a corner ahead. The sounds were probably a group of people coming the other way. Gowli was puzzled – the voices they could hear were sharp, the orders and arguments of people organising themselves, rather than the conversation of a group of companions. They turned the corner, then heard a great crash behind then – a huge boulder had been dropped into the ravine behind them. Hesteon leapt forward. The donkey reared up and Gowli was thrown to the ground. Hesteon, holding tight to the donkey's rope turned round for Gowli and saw that the valley behind them had been blocked by the boulder. Crashing sounds in front and to the sides of them made Hesteon look forward again, to see four men leaping down the sides of the ravine towards them, armed with wooden clubs. Gowli lay on the ground dazed from her fall as the men came towards them. They spread wide in front of Hesteon and kept coming forward threateningly with their clubs.

44

The men were part of the military reserve, travelling to join the muster of Bayronite troops, but they had seen Gowli and Hesteon struggling up the gully. They could see by their clothes and appearance that these were probably Fethonites, and at present Fethonites were fair game. No-one would care about them, hence they had set up the ambush. It was a chance to both attack some Fethonites and make a bit by taking anything they carried, as well as taking the donkey. As the first came close and attempted to bring the club down on Hesteon's head, Hesteon stepped smartly to the side and lashed out with his fist. He felt his hand smash into the face of his assailant. He felt the man crumple under the force of blow. As Hesteon threw the punch, the other men were leaping towards him, aiming blows at him with their clubs. The last Hesteon remembered was feeling his knuckles connect with his assailant's head. After that, all was blackness.

Consciousness was returning to Hesteon. As he woke up he also felt the pain coming to him. The back of his head was excruciatingly painful, as were his knuckles. As awareness returned to him he began to take in other things as well. The smell of cooking. The smell of flowers. The smell of animals. He slowly eased himself onto his elbows and tried to open his eyes.

A firm but gentle woman's voice spoke to him. "Steady, my friend, steady". Hesteon slumped back down onto the bed under the gentle pressure of a hand put to his chest. Hesteon lay back, unresisting. As he lay there, events, as much as he might remember, came back to him. The journey. The donkey. Gowli. The ravine.... He had no idea how long he had been unconscious.

Hesteon again pulled himself to his elbows and opened his eyes. "Gowli – is she all right" he whispered.

Again the woman's voice spoke. "If you mean your friend, she is here." Hesteon looked to where the arm pointed. The woman's voice continued. "She is very poorly, she is badly injured, but we will look after her".

Hesteon turned to look to the other side of his bed, where the voice came from. His eyes met a woman in her mid forties. Not tall, but slim and showing a strength in her being. Her hair was black but cut very short. She wore a long simple robe, brown in colour, with a hood that covered part of her head. Her eyes looked to him with great compassion. The lady's voice continued. "We found you yesterday evening in a ravine, badly injured. You had been beaten and robbed, so we brought you here. Sadly too many people are attacked and robbed in our country".

Hesteon was puzzled – she talked about "we" but there was only her. She was dressed very differently from other women he had seen in his own country or in Bayron. "Where...."

The woman's face suddenly smiled, radiating warmth. "You are in a house on the edge of Gresk. We are a group dedicated to helping the sick, injured. Some call us the Koino Group. Others call us The Commune. My name is Hansa. A messenger told us where you were, so some of us went and carried you here. It is now early morning. You are welcome here."

Hesteon was suddenly inquisitive. "How many? What are you about? Why are you here?" But then his memory leapt back to more immediate issues.

"And Gowli...?" whispered Hesteon.

The woman's face suddenly turned very serious. "She is very badly injured. We do not know if she will survive...."

Over the next couple of days Hesteon's health recovered quickly. His early anger also abated – the anger that people would attack an elderly woman with arthritis, abated by the sense of oneness in the group of people he was living amongst. By the end of the first day he was out of bed, by the beginning of the next he was eating and walking normally. In those 24 hours he had found out much more about the commune. This group of ladies – about 12 of them – was both revered by the Bayronites and disliked by them. Revered for the heroic work they did helping beggars, the injured, the homeless, yet at the same time others disliked and mistrusted them because they helped everyone – Bayronite and non-Bayronite equally. Their philosophy – all are equal, all equally in need.

The group lived in the two-room building, both rooms of a good size. One was used for hospitality and had 6 or 8 beds around the edge – the room where Gowli and Hesteon slept. The other was where the women slept. The two rooms were linked by the corridor with store rooms off, and the cooking area outside to the front of the building. The commune had been built on a slight rise in the middle of one of the shanty areas to the north of Gresk; the building was surrounded by vegetable gardens in a circle about forty yards around the building; in one corner was tethered a donkey that the commune used to shop, carry the sick, take surplus produce to market. By the front door of the building was a bench. Beyond all the grounds was a low fence. If you looked out of the window on one end of the building you looked directly into countryside – at trees, a couple of small fields, a stream, a farmstead. At the other you seemed to look directly into the town. Hesteon noticed the massive city walls a hundred yards away, then noticed the palace towering high above the town. Hesteon also noticed the shanty houses, the market, the shops between the house and the city walls visible from the slightly raised position the house held. The building really did sit on the border of the city and country.

As Hesteon recovered so he did small tasks in and around the house, particularly with nursing Gowli who remained unconscious, although her breathing was even. She had a nasty gash on the brow of her forehead, as well as on her arm and back. Her joints were also swollen – the shock of the attack had triggered off a reaction in her arthritis. Sometimes he thought of why he was there, but had no idea of what he should do. All he could do was care for Gowli whose obstinacy had got him here.

It was towards the end of the second day that the leader of the women asked Hesteon to sit with her on the bench at the front of the building. Hansa was a small rounded lady, a lady of strength but whose eyes would readily twinkle with humour. Hesteon knew as Hansa because that was the name she used when she introduced herself, but most in the group called her mother.

Hansa was a remarkable lady, certainly if the things that the other women told him were true. She seemed to have darker skin than most, but she was lively, alert, with eyes that missed nothing. It was on her energy that this commune had been built, and many others would have joined her. She had chosen these twelve because they alone seemed to her the people who would give, and not count the cost, who would give, and not ask to whom they were giving. Even if you did not know, you would have guessed that she was the leader of the group.

Hansa clearly had questions she wanted to ask. "My friend, it is rare to find a middle aged man and an older woman travelling from an alien land to this city for no apparent reason." Hansa's eyes twinkled with humour as she spoke. "It is even rarer to find such a couple travelling in such troubled times as these. Do you have a story you would like to tell me?".

Hesteon hesitated, so Hansa continued, much more seriously. "You do not have to tell me anything, but if we are to help you we need to know what help you need". Still Hesteon looked confused and hesitated. Hansa explained again. "We can heal your bodies, but the help you need is far deeper than that. The help you need is not for your body but for your spirit. We will help you if you tell us how".

Hesteon at last found the words he had been searching for. "I do not think it is good for any of us to tell you my story."

Hansa and Hesteon sat there quietly saying nothing. The quiet seemed to stretch into minutes, but Hesteon knew he hadn't been dismissed, that Hansa still wanted him there. At last he glanced at Hansa and was surprised at what he saw. Hansa was crying. "What...."

Hansa looked at Hesteon. "I am crying because I too can feel the deep deep pain of your heart. I can feel the deep pain of your friend in the other room. I am crying because you are in despair. I shed tears for the burden you carry alone".

Hesteon felt the emotion flood over him and felt the tears washing down his own cheeks. It was the first time he had cried since Teon had been taken. Hansa pulled Hesteon to her and held him as he wept tears, all the tears he had not wept for Teon, for Janci, for the events of the last two weeks.

At last the tears subsided. He began to speak. He told of Janci and her death. He told of Hamlan and his murder. He told her of Teon, his son, the good lad, who had confessed to the murder. He told her of his feelings when he heard that the Emperor had been killed and Teon accused. He told her of Gowli, and how she alone had kept faith in Teon. He told of their journey to Gresk to try and see Teon once more. He told how he knew Teon would die, yet just once he had to see him – his only link to Janci whom he had adored. Hesteon held nothing back. Hansa said nothing but listened. At the end of Hesteon's tale both sat in silence on the bench for several minutes. At last Hansa spoke briefly. "We will help you. You must remain here. I will tell no-one what you have told me." She stood and returned to the house, leaving Hesteon on the bench.

For Teon one day seemed to drift into another. The pain. His hunger. The cold and damp of the cell. His cough. His broken arm, hurting a little less now. The bruising on his face, on the rest of his body. Only one thing had changed – what was happening outside the window of his cell. Although he couldn't see clearly out of his window because it was well above his head, he had worked out that his cell window opened onto a big courtyard, and he could hear that huge preparations were taking place in the courtyard. Teon guessed they were probably for the Emperor's funeral.

Before now he had not been aware of anything else, but now there was one thing he did notice. He could just glimpse a stone tower, perhaps the tallest tower around the courtyard, at what may have been the far side of the courtyard. Since the Emperor had died it had changed. A lamp had been lit at the top of it, and was kept lit for 24 hours a day. The lamp was a calling to mourning for everyone in the castle and the city below.

The light flickered – it was clearly a burning flame – bringing both light and a sense of movement into Teon's consciousness making a contrast to the awful stillness and despair of his cell. Sometimes the light seemed to be barely there, barely burning. The light burnt and showed best in the darkness. Teon nicknamed it 'the dark light', and it gave him a remarkable degree of comfort. Until now all had been darkness, pain, suffering, cough, hurt. Here the "dark light" gave him a simple glimpse of life in his living death.

7

The city of Gresk was abuzz: all were excited that the day of the Emperor's funeral had finally arrived. Some were excited because it was a day off work, some excited because of the number of dignitaries and colour in the city, others because they had truly respected the Emperor Pellaig and felt affection and respect for the Empress in her mourning.

It was the morning after Hesteon had broken into tears and told everything to Hansa. Surprisingly he slept really well for the first time for over three weeks. He woke early, and went to Gowli. He sat down with her, listening to her soft-breathing. In the two days of being here she had lost a lot of weight through not eating, and her cheeks had sunk into her head. He noticed too that her eyes were looking as if they too were about to sink into her forehead. But he noticed something different this morning – there was a restlessness about her as she lay on the bed. She had been still the night before, and over the previous days, but now she was moving, her legs and arms twisting, her head rocking from side to side.

Suddenly Gowli, in one movement, sat bolt upright, opened her eyes and screamed.

The scream took Hesteon by surprise. Within seconds the women of the Koino group were roused and joined Hesteon. They tried to calm Gowli. They tried to ease her back onto the bed. They spoke to her soothingly, but Gowli was sitting rigidly, seeing no-one. However her screaming ended as sharply as it started.

Suddenly she turned her head, looked straight at Hesteon and spoke in a shrill voice. "They will kill him today". With that, Gowli appeared to relax. The women were able to get her to lie on the bed, and in seconds she was again fast asleep.

Hesteon had been so surprised by Gowli's sudden movement and voice that he had not moved at all. Who will kill him?

Who will be killed? What did she know? How did she know? Hesteon turned to Hansa who was still stood next to Gowli. "What...?" he asked in his shock.

Hansa smiled softly, but without humour. She spoke reassuringly: "My friend, this was for us, not you. We must let her sleep." Hesteon could not speak – he remained silent in his confusion.

Magrell also woke knowing that today was to be the funeral. So far all had gone so smoothly. He had got rid of the Emperor and his heir. He had married the Emperor's widow. The council had elected him to be the new Emperor. Yet, Magrell knew that today would be a turning point.

Today, after the funeral, was the day he would declare war on Fethon. He had grounds for declaring war in the shape of the assassin, the boy in the dungeon. He knew that in days he would have mustered his army, invaded Fethon and taken its capital, Durringham. In two weeks he would have total control of Fethon as well as Bayron. Of course he would let the Fethonite king return to his people after the funeral so he could defeat him, capture him, humiliate him, execute him in front of his own people, so that he would not be accused of treachery towards a guest. He would ensure that the Fethonite king could say nothing at the funeral – he was aware of Jayron's growing reputation and that Jayron might produce something to turn the prevailing anti-Fethon atmosphere in a different direction. Letting Jayron return and then killing him – it was a good way to cower a people and deter any possible rebellions – the sight of their own king tortured and executed. Today would be the day when the invasion campaign would begin.

Magrell's mind also wandered to the boy in the cells deep below in the palace. He would also take the boy, perhaps in the next few days, and execute him, publicly, to show his ruthlessness to anyone who dared to cross him.

Of course, thought Magrell, today would also be the day when he would start his reign officially, when he would start enjoying his rule over the Bayronites. Until now he had had to show he was in mourning for the Emperor, and show his respect for Haren the Emperor's wife, but after the funeral he could show his iron fist. Within a few days Ganerr would have disappeared, dead, never to be seen again. Within weeks those members of the council who had voted against him would also be removed, some murdered to frighten the others. He smiled as he remembered Haren. He would allow her to live. The letter gave him complete control over her. The letter had left her totally defeated. The moment he wanted rid of her, if that need arose, he would simply produce the letter as if he had just found it, and have her executed for treason. Within weeks there would be no-one left to defy him. Magrell would rule totally, ruthlessly and completely. There would be no opposition.

Magrell left his chamber – it was the day of the funeral and he had some business to see to. The funeral was later but there were details to sort out.

Jayron also knew that this was the day of the funeral. Since his arrival a few days before, Jayron and his generals had kept themselves to their quarters, as sparse as they were. Jayron requested on a number of occasions to meet Teon but had not been granted the request. He had not pushed the matter because he did not want to create a diplomatic incident. He and his generals also discussed when they should leave, immediately after the funeral itself, or later after the mourning feast, or perhaps the next day. At times they wondered whether they would be allowed to leave at all.

The party had, on occasions left their quarters and walked in the grounds of the palace. Each time they had remained dignified in the face of threats and insults. Each time they were accompanied by Bayronite soldiers. Magrell called them guides, but they were clearly there to guard them. Once Jayron wanted to leave the palace but the "guides" had simply stood blocking his way, saying it was for his own safety, or that it was too dangerous.

Jayron and his generals were still discussing when to leave when there was a knock. They opened the door to see Magrell standing there.

Magrell walked in, full of confidence. "Friends", he said. "Today you will be honoured guests at the funeral of the Emperor. You will have special seats, and I must request you to take up the seats in a few moments. However, I also have a further request to make of you."

The Fethonite party said nothing – Magrell spoke in a tone that suggested he should not be denied. He continued. "I believe it is right for your party to leave immediately after the funeral. Our soldiers will guide you out of the city, to the border. It would not be appropriate to let you attend the funeral feast this evening. At the border your escort will give you a letter of greeting for your parliament. We hope the letter strengthens...", Magrell's tone was suddenly very sarcastic "...strengthens the ties between our two countries."

As soon as he finished speaking, Magrell turned and left. Guards came a few minutes later and lead the Fethonite party into the courtyard for the funeral, seating them on chairs specially erected for the occasion.

After the sudden waking early in the morning Gowli slept for perhaps three hours. Hesteon sat with her all through those hours to about mid morning. It was about then, when Gowli began to stir again. This time Gowli returned to consciousness much more slowly, much more painfully. Gowli could feel all her joints hurting – she easily recognised the arthritic pain. She could feel the gash and bruising on her head and back. She woke slowly, opening her eyes one at a time as if trying them out for the first time. The sight of Gowli regaining some semblance of consciousness caused Hesteon's spirits to leap. As Gowli roused he sat by the bed holding her hand.

When she was sufficiently awake Hesteon put a cup of water to Gowli's lips and she drank slowly but readily. Gowli continued to lie on the bed with Hesteon sat on a stool beside her, Hesteon reassuring her, holding her hand. Gowli tried to moved but couldn't – the injuries she had received and the arthritic reaction prevented that. Gowli tried to speak but found that impossible as well. The two remained together for the rest of the day, Hesteon holding Gowli's hand as the women of the commune and the city-folk did their duty – mourning the death of their Emperor.

The funeral followed the pattern of most state funerals. Magrell made sure the best possible funeral had been arranged. The funeral had plenty of pomp. The coffin had been carried in to the courtyard of the palace on a carriage pulled by ten horses after being paraded around the city, accompanied by 200 horsemen. The city dwellers lined the streets in silence to pay their respects. Magrell, as well as others, gave eulogies for the Emperor. Haren was genuinely saddened at the event. There were fanfares, singing, soldiers marching around in slow march. Jayron knew that if nothing else these events were very long and very boring.

Finally the coffin was taken to the great bonfire that had been built on the raised stone platform at the far end of the courtyard. The coffin was placed in the middle. The bonfire was lit. All remained, as the coffin and body were burnt – it was the Bayronite custom for dead Emperors and dignitaries.

At last the funeral was over. Magrell and other Bayronite leaders were led out towards the mourning banquet. Visiting dignitaries from other countries also followed into the great banqueting hall. After a few minutes there was no-one in the courtyard but the Fethonite delegation. A Soldier came over and spoke formally and icily.

"Sir, your escort to the border is waiting for you".

Jayron thanked the soldier in a tone much warmer than he had just received. He and his companions returned to their horses, loaded their packs and in minutes were riding south accompanied by a troop of Bayronite cavalry.

That evening Hesteon was still sitting with Gowli who seemed to have dropped into some twilight existence between consciousness and unconsciousness, waking and sleep. Through the day she had taken water but did not take any food. She also appeared to be in a lot of pain and discomfort, but Hesteon could do little to ease her suffering.

After the women of the commune returned from the Emperor's funeral, Hesteon noticed that they spent a lot of time in their own room in conversation. The talking was deliberately quiet to prevent anyone else hearing. Hesteon instinctively knew he was excluded from the meeting.

It was about twilight when Hansa came to him. Hansa sat beside Hesteon and put her hand on his as he held Gowli's hand. After a few moments Hansa spoke to him.

"Hesteon". She spoke very quietly. No-one else could have heard even if they were trying to hear. "Hesteon, tonight we will help you, although it may be some days before you are able to see what is happening. Do not worry, but some of us will be gone awhile." With that she was gone. Later in the minutes after dusk he heard a number of the women leaving the commune. He was certain they were heading towards the city.

Jayron guessed that they would be safe returning to Fethon. He guessed, rightly, that Magrell would want a much more spectacular end to the Fethonite royal family, and he certainly would not want to be linked to treachery towards guests. Magrell would want to make Jayron's death into a spectacular event to humiliate the Fethonite people. Jayron also guessed that Magrell thought he was militarily much stronger than the Fethonite people, and he could take Fethon when he wanted. Jayron reviewed in his mind the strength of the Fethonite defences and knew that Magrell was undoubtedly right – his standing army may well be five times as big as that of Fethon, and if the reserves were called up, perhaps even ten times as big.

The party rode at a trot to the border, arriving at dusk. At the border the leader of the guard presented Jayron with the letter Magrell had promised him. Jayron and his group rode on while the guards returned along the path they had come. It was only when he came within a few miles of Durringham that he read the letter, reading it aloud to the party with him.

"From Magrell, Emperor of Bayron, Lord of the northern Lands, Master of Gresk," – Jayron read with just a hint of irony in his voice. "To the people of Fethon. We now have evidence that Jayron and the leaders of your people have plotted to kill our Emperor and his heir and to take over our land, and have partly succeeded in their evil plan. They have done this through an agent – a young man called Teon. This is an act of war that we cannot ignore. A cost has to be paid. We demand that you, as a nation, submit and pay tribute to us, and within the next three months become part of the mighty Bayronite empire. Further we demand that you hand over Jayron and his co-leaders" – Jayron read out a list of about 20 names: all the leading figures of Fethon – "for punishment and execution." If you do not follow this path voluntarily within 7 days, then we will invade your country as we have the right to do for such an act of betrayal, obviously having to leave widespread bloodshed in our path, and still fulfilling the task that we need to do of assuming your country into our empire. Friends, to put it bluntly, submit, or be conquered by our vastly superior army."

Jayron raised an eyebrow. " Friends" he said with understatement and a hollow smile on his face, "I think we have a problem".

8

As all mourning feasts, the event began solemnly until the alcohol began to flow. About two hundred and fifty people packed into the banqueting hall and ate in silence at first. The murmur of conversation barely rose loudly enough to drown the sound of the wind blowing outside.

After the first couple of courses of the feast the ale and spirits began to flow and the men drank freely. The volume of noise increased as the drink flowed, and as the drink flowed so the feast was overtaken by the laughter of those who were there. For two hours, maybe three those partaking in the banquet ate and drank, Magrell among them. Now that the funeral was over and his rule cemented, Magrell felt he could relax for the first time in weeks, he felt free to drink rather more generously, he did not feel the need to keep such a clear head as he had until now.

However, Magrell also knew what he needed to do as Emperor – he knew that good Emperors had to be strong and unyielding if they were to rule, if his rule were to last. Of course ruthlessness had to be tempered by generosity: he must be seen to be more generous than his predecessor. He knew that only his generosity combined with fear would bring the personal loyalty he would need, and indeed craved, from both his own people and from neighbouring states.

At last the food, the drinking and the laughing had run their course. Magrell stood to his feet and quietened the room. "Friends". He began his speech. "Friends, I thank you for your support at this time of great national mourning. I especially thank those who have travelled from afar to be here. I thank you for joining us to remember our great Emperor, so sadly and brutally brought to an end of his life." Magrell lifted his glass as if drinking a toast to his visitors.

"This is a sad day" he continued, "for the country of Bayron, betrayed by a neighbouring king and state whom we considered friends, a state we have given considerable help and friendship to. Friends, we have been betrayed by the nation of Fethon, and particularly the king of Fethon who sent an agent, a boy, to try to destroy our country. Jayron – too cowardly to fight himself – sent a boy of maybe 15 years to do his dirty work. My friends," Magrell was in full voice. "You are here today to note that I have challenged Fethon to give up their cowardly leaders to face punishment for their crimes. If they do not do that – and I have given them seven days – then we are at war with Fethon, and the consequences of that war is theirs."

The pitch and tone of Magrell's speech rose as he spoke. His confidence grew as the effects of the alcohol and power he now knew he wielded grew within him. As Magrell paused in his speech, the people at the banquet – both his own people and the visitors from other lands – rose to their feet applauding and cheering. Carried along by the drink and the passionate words, they knew Magrell had chosen the right course.

When the noise had abated, Magrell continued. "Friends, loyal citizens of Bayron, I urge you to prepare for war. Friends from other countries, we thank you for your support. We thank you for sharing with us in our sadness. We thank you for understanding the situation we are in". Magrell knew that not one of the delegates would oppose what he had arranged to do, not one would stand for Fethon. Even more, the delegates from other countries would be cowed by the Bayronites for the future – Magrell's ambition, growing in the previous few days, went far beyond the uniting of Bayron and Fethon.

"Finally, my friends, I would like you to see the sort of weapons they are using in Fethon." Magrell, his mind clouded with drink, had forgotten his notion to take Teon back to Fethon for execution. He turned to the guards and spoke sharply. "Bring the boy here".

For Teon the day passed as all the others. A fitful night's sleep, disturbed by the coughing and pain whenever he moved. Constantly, when awake in the night, he stared at the light and found strength in its light and life. Earlier his bread and water had come. He had spent the day listening as much as he could to the events in the courtyard. Clearly a great solemn state occasion was taking place, almost certainly the funeral of the Emperor. In the evening the guards had brought him more food, the "trusty" had come to change the bucket. As dusk came on, Teon looked hard at the dark light shining on the tower, somehow giving him strength in his weakness.

This night the light seemed to shine brighter, seemed to flicker more. As he watched he felt something say in his head "I am with you". The thought was gone in an instant. Teon wrapped himself in his blankets and lay on the floor to sleep.

But for Teon, the sleep never arrived. He made himself as comfortable as possible After lying down Teon's cough would take over and rack his body for many minutes and this evening was no different. As the cough subsided, he heard sounds outside the door. He heard voices talking, then keys rattling in his cell door.

Teon's heart started to beat faster – he knew this was something different. The door swung fully open. Four guards entered the room and roughly hauled Teon to his feet. Teon felt his bruises, felt his broken arm scream out in pain although his weakened chest didn't allow him to voice the scream. The guards didn't notice, or didn't care about, Teon's agony as they led him out of the cell. One guard walked in front, two held him, the other walked behind as they headed along the corridor, turned the corner at the end, headed along another corridor and through a thick wooden door. Teon's legs felt weak as he walked with the guards. Through his mind ran the thought that someone had spoken to him. Had said to him "I am with you". He did not know who or what – there had been nothing tangible in his cell. He just knew that he had found a glimmer of strength in the darkness of the world he was inhabiting. He also feared that this could be the end – his execution may be just around the corner.

They took Teon through another corridor, then another. Sometimes he had to climb a set of stairs. Once or twice he had to go down a set. Teon was soon disorientated and breathing heavily, although the guards wouldn't stop to allow him time to recover.

After an age, the small party stopped by a large wooden door on the side of the corridor – a wide corridor, well lit – light that caused Teon's eyes to hurt, the first corridor where Teon had seen other people walking along. It seemed to be a corridor to the kitchens, as men and women walked along carrying dishes, empty goblets and wine jugs, others carrying full jugs of wine and ale, trays with bread. All carefully avoided Teon's eye; indeed, pretended he didn't exist at all. Teon knew they were deliberately looking the other way.

One of the guards walked further along the corridor, then disappeared through a door. A few moments later the door in front of Teon was swung open.

The light from the door dazzled Teon, and for a few moments left him feeling blinded. The weeks in the dark cell had had an impact on his eyes, leaving them far more sensitive than they had been. He felt the guards pushing him forward into the room. He heard the hundreds of people in the room before his eyes could adjust enough to see them. He heard a voice speaking that he had heard before.

"Boy", the voice that Teon recognised said, "come and stand on this platform". Teon was pushed up a set of steps, then stood on a stone platform. He looked a pathetic sight: thin, hair unkempt and just a bit too long, a wispy beard forming on his chin, his clothes grubby and torn, his arm in a splint, his feet bare, the yellow of the receding bruise on his face. He stood there, his sight returning. As he became more aware of his surroundings he could see that all the eyes, hundreds of eyes, in the room were on him.

Magrell continued, this time with a mocking tone in his voice. "Friends, this is the sort of weapon that Fethon is using now". The room laughed. Again Magrell knew clearly that he could reinforce the justice of his cause with mockery of the enemy. Magrell viciously caught hold of Teon's hair and pulled his face up for everyone to see. "Fethon – the country where the boys are braver than the men". Again the room laughed in drunken mockery, as Magrell continued with the confidence of drink. "Surely a king who sends this sort of dross to fight for him is the greatest yellow-bellied coward this world knows and deserves all that we will give him." As he spoke sarcastically Magrell made a chopping motion with his arm an action he continued as the room cheered even more loudly. After the hubbub died down, Magrell allowed a long silence to develop. "Friends", he continued, this time with a vicious tone to his voice "This is the one who killed our Emperor. Who killed his son. Who tried to destroy our nation. I want revenge for our great leader."

Magrell quickly and unexpectedly turned and swung a punch at Teon's head which caught him just by his eye and knocked Teon to the floor. Teon looked up and his eyes caught the window at the far end of the room, the light burning outside. The voice again, "I am with you always". The voice was gone just as fleetingly as Magrell took a kick at the body on the floor. And another. And another. Teon felt the boot in the pit of his stomach, then making contact with his head. The men in the room cheered drunkenly. Magrell pulled Teon to his feet by his hair, and as quickly punched him to the ground and lashed out again with his boot. Teon had no idea how often he had been kicked, although another kick landed on his broken arm and gave him excruciating pain. Long before Magrell's frenzied attack came to an end Teon passed into unconsciousness. He finished an unconscious, slight and bloodied heap on the floor, a symbol of Magrell's style of leadership. Everyone knew no-one in that condition could survive such a beating. No one dared move the body.

Long after the feast Teon's body still lay on the platform where he had been beaten. In his drunkenness Magrell had left him on the stage for the rest of the feast as a symbol for everyone of his ruthlessness. Magrell, and everyone else, thought him dead. Teon's breath was coming very faintly, his heart struggling to beat on. At the end of the feast Magrell had turned to the head servant and spoke shortly: "dispose of it", he said, nodding towards the lifeless heap.

The head servant called four of the female servants who picked up the body and carried it out of the banqueting room. The head servant led them into the service corridor along which Teon had earlier been brought to the banquet. The servants carried the body along for perhaps forty yards towards the kitchen, then stopped. The head servant waited until no-one else was in the corridor, then unlocked and opened a small door. The four female servants slipped through the door with the body. The door was quickly closed and locked again behind them. No-one saw them disappear. Only the head servant knew that these servants were not employed at the palace.

9

Two mornings later Gowli still clung on, sleeping much, sometimes conscious, sometimes able to hold a simple conversation with Hesteon. Despite Hesteon gently questioning her, Gowli had no memory of her sudden outburst. The women of the commune still worked to keep her comfortable and to keep Hesteon fed and recovering himself. Gowli occasionally took a drink of water, a little soup, but nothing else to eat. Hesteon knew that although she kept going at the moment she could not survive this much longer. There would have to be some sort of miracle for Gowli to survive.

Hesteon also sensed a change in the atmosphere of the commune. Now the women of the commune were busier, worried, absorbed with something else. During Hesteon's time at the commune one or two others were brought in to receive the care the women provided, staying in the same room as Hesteon and Gowli. Often Hesteon would minister to their needs as he could. However, since the day of the Emporer's funeral Hesteon had seen changes in the commune – the door to the women's quarters kept shut, a constant supply of warm water being taken into the other room, bloodstained cloths hanging to dry. It was obvious that there was someone else in the commune, being kept in the other room. Hesteon guessed that whomever it was had arrived, presumably brought in, very late two nights before when Hesteon and Gowli were asleep. The women of the commune were making sure that neither Hesteon nor anyone else could see him or her, but he knew that whoever it was, was causing them considerable worry and work.

Frequently Hesteon asked about the person in the other room, and at first the women simply denied there was anyone else. However Hesteon persisted, until Hansa had just said – "please don't ask because I will not tell you. It is too dangerous for you to know. He is a very important person, but a fugitive."

At one stage, a few hours later, Hansa took Hesteon to sit on the bench. She explained to him that she could say nothing, but that he had to trust them. He was to do nothing, but he was to trust that they were helping. Hansa would say no more. Several times Hesteon wondered, and even asked if he could help, but had been firmly kept out of the other room, his questions unanswered. All he knew by the one slip of the tongue – it was a man. As he nursed Gowli the question twisted around his mind – what on earth is happening here? Who is the person in the next room?

Magrell knew that Fethon would never give in to his demands – no country would do that. National pride, love for their leader, call it what you want, but every country believed they could stand firm against the world. Even before the funeral Magrell had begun to prepare his country for the invasion of Fethon. He had sent messengers to all the reserve leaders telling them to mobilise their troops, to begin the process of raising arms. After the funeral the process had sped up, and the army was gathering in the fields around Gresk. Magrell's standing army, mostly troops on horseback, had already begun to move towards the border with Fethon. The volunteer and reserve armies were preparing weapons and supplies. After a few days commandeered carts were used to move the forces and their equipment towards the border with Fethon. Fethon was only five hours from Gresk and it was only a matter of days, after the muster in the fields that the invading troops were on the border of Fethon.

Magrell's instincts told him that he had to play this game legitimately – he would give the Fethonites the seven days as he promised. The country would not survive the eighth.

Jayron spent the first three days at home, after the funeral, meeting with his councillors. They had discussed all the alternatives. Jayron had even considered giving himself up, but knew that would not save the country. They would still have to submit, and within a short time the persecution would begin, and he knew how an occupying dictatorship worked – invasion, persecution, then executions would start soon afterwards as the country was raped of all its wealth and culture.

Jayron and his councillors also discussed the possibility of defending the country and mustered their own troops. Jayron was also well aware that his troops were far fewer in number than the Bayronites could muster, and his cities had walls that would not stand up to the Bayronite forces. Jayron's intelligence also confirmed what he suspected: that the armies of Bayron, already amassed on his border, were far more powerful, far better armed, than the Fethonites. Jayron remained confident on the surface, but underneath knew his army, even embattled in their own country, were no match for the Bayronites.

As much as they talked, Jayron could see no alternative that could save his country, that could save his people.

At the commune it was now the third morning. Gowli still struggled on, Hesteon nursing her. Hesteon also sensed by a slight change in atmosphere that the stranger in the other room had perhaps pulled through the worse – at least he hadn't died – and he could hear him occasionally groaning in pain. Over the last day he had felt the atmosphere lighten amongst the women of the commune. He could sense that their hopes for the stranger had risen.

Later in the day, Hansa invited Hesteon to sit on the bench with her. It was clear that she had something special to share with him. Hansa did not wait, but began speaking as soon as they had sat down.

"You may be wondering" she started slowly, "about the stranger in the other room". Her eye glinted for a moment to show she had been aware of Hesteon's questions and enquiring looks. "When he was brought here...", she hesitated "When we brought him here he had been very badly beaten. We did not think that he would live, but the human body is a remarkable thing, Hesteon." Hansa looked at the floor as she spoke. "He is a very special person, chosen for a great task." Hesteon's mind was beginning to churn with even more questions – chosen by whom? For what? Who was He?

Hansa ignored Hesteon's confusion and continued to speak. "Today at this stage we know that he will probably live. We know that in about three days he may be able to travel, although he will have to ride on our donkey." Hansa hesitated before continuing:

"Well, not so much may be able to travel – he will have to travel. He will not be able to walk very far, if at all." Hesteon was still wondering what all this was about and why she was telling him this as if it was the most important thing he had to hear.

Hansa was still talking to the floor. "He has to travel to Fethon. He must return to Fethon as soon as he is able. He has been chosen for a special task".

"What special task?" asked Hesteon.

"It is not for you..." Hansa paused, "...or I to know, but he must return, and..." Hansa paused again, "...And you must take him, Hesteon".

Hesteon started. "Me?"

Hansa was now suddenly very firm as she turned and looked straight in his face. "Yes, you. You must take him to Fethon." Hesteon was confused – he had to stay with Gowli, he had to stay here. He could not return. He could not take someone back to Fethon. Now. Hansa spoke again: "Hesteon, come with me!"

Hesteon stood to his feet, hesitantly, and followed Hansa into the communal room from where he had been excluded for three days. Hansa beckoned him over to a bed in the far corner of the room, where he could make out a crumpled heap that was a person lying down. Hansa directed him to the bed with her hand.

At first Hesteon couldn't make out much of the stranger. He was slight, thin. His hair was dishevelled and he had a thin untidy beard. He was bruised, his face badly cut, his arm clearly badly damaged, as well as fingers broken and tied crudely in splints. The lower half of his body was hidden under the covers. Hesteon looked again and sudden realisation dawned on him. He was looking at the face of his son. Teon's eyes looked back at him.

Hansa left Hesteon alone for a few moments with Teon. Hesteon passed through a multitude of feelings in seconds. Anger at whoever had done this. Anger at Teon for causing all this change and upheaval in life. Concern. A fatherly instinct to protect. Even the hunter's instinct to kill a wounded animal. And most – complete helplessness and incomprehension at what was going on. Hesteon also noticed there was something different here.

Something about Teon had changed, but what? It took him several minutes to realise – there was something different about his eyes. He looked into Teon's eyes and saw a fire burning he had never seen before. A fire burning he was sure had never been there before. As Hesteon stared at his son, those eyes looking back at him, Hansa returned.

"Hesteon! Hesteon!" Hansa repeated his name firmly several times until he looked at her. "There are two things to be done". Hesteon still looked on with confusion. "Hesteon, there is someone he must meet. Then as soon as possible, perhaps even in two days, he must return to Fethon. Come!"

Hansa took control and led Hesteon into the other room where Gowli was lying still on the bed. Hansa whispered something to her, then pulled back the covers and lifted her up in her arms. Gowli was little more than skin and bone, weighing less than a child. Hansa carried Gowli carefully through to the next room and lay her on the bed beside Teon. Both were awake, both looking at each other, into each other's eyes, both hardly able to speak. Hesteon was about to move to them but Hansa held out her hand. It was Gowli who spoke first.

"Teon, did you do it?" Her voice was barely a whisper.

Teon's voice was even quieter in his reply. "No".

Gowli lay there for a few moments her eyes smiling softly at the answer. She and Teon looked into each other's eyes as they both lay on the bed, both in their respective suffering. Then Gowli whispered again, her voice even quieter. "Farewell, chosen one". She closed her eyes, never to open them again.

It was a dark, clear night – the only light came from the moon that cast eerie shadows on the ground. The small group of people, dressed in coarse cloaks and hoods, moved quietly and confidently under the shelter of the rock face and tied their donkeys and goats with long reins to a single tree. In the group were men and women, a younger girl and a number of children, perhaps twenty in total. Few others saw these people; those who did described them as wild, barbaric, primitive, of limited speech. These were north people, those who lived in the mountainous and forested regions to the north of Bayron and Fethon. Even now they were further south than they would normally travel.

Few knew the origins of the north people. Most assumed they were a separate race, their skin being a darker colour than the southern peoples. It wasn't true – around five hundred years before, a group of Fethonites had fled a ruthless king who had wanted to take over their homesteads and take their daughters for a harem. They had fled north, and it was their descendants who were now the fierce nomadic people known as the north people. As the refugees had adapted to living in the harsh environment, so they had found complex speech less important to them, their language had been reduced to short abrupt phrases.

Wandering, hunting for food, collecting edible plants, stockherding, camping at places like this in the night, setting up camp by moonlight, was their chosen lifestyle. This group had about a dozen camping grounds they used, but they rarely stayed more than two or three days in any one place. There were many similar groups – called clans – who sometimes joined together, sometimes went their separate ways.

The group were skilled at their camping. Putting up shelters by moonlight was easy if the ground was familiar – tonight it was – they had camped here at the southernmost of their sites a number of times before. The group was also highly skilled at building fires. They knew to collect kindling and some firewood in the late afternoon and carry it with them to their site, so that in the darkness they did not have to search for the means of getting the fire going. This night it was no different.

Within half an hour they had pitched their tents, led their animals to grazing and lit the fire. Within an hour they had cooked and eaten the six rabbits they had caught earlier – more than enough for the eighteen people in the clan.

The clan had travelled almost all the day to reach this point and were weary with the travel. The Mother of the clan – the clan leader's wife – Angala had insisted they travel to the south of their territory. She didn't know why, but they had to go south. Direction had little consequence for them, so the rest of the clan, including the clan leader Comp, her husband, had been happy to go with her. Hence they had reached the most southerly of their camping sites under the cliff face.

When all had been prepared, the food eaten, Comp called the clan to the circle. The circle was one of the traditions of the north people. The clan gathered each evening, sat in a circle around the fire and held hands. Comp released one of his hands, took a cup of water and drank. He passed it to Angala, and she too drank. The water was passed from person to person, each taking a drink from the carved wooden cup, carved with patterns of flames and faces intermingled with each other. After passing the cup to the next person in the circle each person held hands again with the people next to them.

The tradition after the cup of water was simply to sit around the fire, holding hands until the flames had died. Each sat with their own thoughts. But tonight was different. Suddenly Angala stood. The circle was never broken: this was unique. All looked to her as she began to speak quietly. "See face. Chosen one come. Prepare him. Clan here. Him walk. We meet. Go to Golo. Prepare Golo." Angala was silent for what seemed an age, all eyes watching her as she stood in the light of the fire. She walked across the circle to the young girl who was perhaps fourteen years old, her daughter Anga. She raised Anga to her feet and held her daughter's face in her hands. She looked deeply into Anga's eyes, then spoke directly to her, though all heard. "Golo. Go. Find darkness. Golo your gift." Angala took Anga in her arms and hugged her hard, then returned to her place, sat again and reformed the circle, all holding hands. All felt excited. Cheered. All were elated to hear of a chosen one, but said nothing. All knew that there would be special work to do the next day. That night, all were happy to be in the circle. There had never been a chosen one for their clan before.

Hesteon stayed in the room for several minutes, staring at his son, crying for Gowli. She had been so special. She had really been his own mother in all except blood. He had never been aware before this moment of how good Gowli was. He was discovering that goodness was in the fire of an old woman, not in the respectability of a village elder. After a few minutes Hansa returned and led Hesteon by the hand into the other room. She spoke very firmly to him.

"Hesteon" she said, "This is no time for crying. You must take Teon to Fethon, to Durringham. You must take him to Jayron. You have tomorrow to prepare, but then you must take

Teon. You may shed your tears later, but for now, prepare and go. It is for the sake of all our people."

"But why? How? What will he do?" Confusion had returned to Hesteon.

Hansa replied in her firm voice. "I do not know that. I do not know if Jayron will see him. I do not know if Jayron will be alive. I just know that he must go back, and you must take him". When Hansa was in this mood she was someone who was not to be refused. They both knew there was no more to be said.

Through the next day Hesteon prepared. At times he tried to speak to Teon, but Teon's injuries led him to sleep for long periods. When awake he would listen to his father talking and heard how his father came to be at The Commune. For Teon the accumulated shock of his beatings and time in the cell prevented him from facing or talking of the horrors he had been through since leaving Mayeringham. At the same time Hansa had much for Hesteon to do, leaving the women caring for Teon for much of the day.

Early in the day, Hansa had shown Hesteon the burial plot that belonged to the community. Two of the women helped him, and by late morning Gowli had been buried. Hesteon knew events happening around them would never allow them to return her to her village, if the village even survived. Anyway, with Hesteon and Teon gone there would be no-one left at the village to tend the grave. Hesteon carved a piece of wood for her and put it on her grave. He wrote, "Gowli, a chosen one".

The afternoon was spent rigging up a saddle for the donkey that belonged to the community, a saddle that would hold Teon in place. By using pieces of wood, straps and the donkey saddle Hesteon felt he made something which should carry Teon.

Teon was young and regained some strength through the day. By the end of the day he had eaten solid food, using his less damaged arm, eating without too much pain, although the injuries he had still looked horrific. Before bed Teon had managed to sit up on his own. Hesteon had also collected food for the journey that he put in a knapsack to carry the next day. He knew the journey could take two or three days. Hansa had also made it clear that they would have to avoid the main route from Bayron to Fethon – the Bayronite army was using that route in great numbers at the moment in preparation for the invasion of Fethon. They would have to take the mountain track farther to the north – a harsher, colder, damper, longer route rarely travelled, over the high plateau, but a route which would lead them to Fethon. Only Hansa realised that the cold and damp would be very hard on Teon, but she said nothing.

10

Jayron sought long and hard for a solution, for a way out. His one hope now – to prevent as much bloodshed as possible for his people. He had sent messengers to all the villages on the road towards Bayron, inviting the residents to Durringham to escape the initial drive of the Bayronites into Fethon.

Messengers travelled to Mayeringham, and the residents were more than pleased to have the opportunity to escape the coming onslaught; most had already packed. Many of them had seen the Bayronite army amassing over the border in Bayron, and those who hadn't, had heard descriptions that grew with the telling. Within a day, the village emptied. The residents took what they could, including their livestock and families, and journeyed quickly along the road to Durringham.

One man remained. Bohran, ever since his clash with Gowli, had sat deeper and deeper into his chair, had appeared less and less in the village. He knew Gowli had been right, that his cowardice had stopped him rightfully defending one of his villagers, and worse, had allowed a child to go to his death at the hands of the brutal Bayronite people. He knew that if it hadn't been for his cowardice, if Teon had not been taken to Gresk, it might be that this whole invasion would not be threatened. What appeared initially as a success and an easy way out, had become a great catastrophe for both his village and his country. Bohran summoned up one last ounce of any courage he had, and would not leave. "I will remain and do my duty" he had said to his family as he saw them leave with the rest of the refugees, heading for Durringham. His family left in great sorrow – they were certain they would not see Bohran again.

For Jayron himself, there seemed to be only one possibility: he would take his soldiers – but only his personal guard – out to meet the Bayronites. He would bargain with the Bayronites – he would seek the safety of his people, and offer himself if that was what was needed to save them. He would allow the others named on the letter from Magrell to escape to wherever they chose to go, but he himself would stay and plead for his people. Surely life under the Bayronite heel would be better than death?

Teon learned from Hansa that the next day he would begin his journey to return to Fethon – he too had spent some time talking to her. Through those weeks in the cell and the beatings he had taken, he had never believed he would live, let alone see his land again. The thought of the journey horrified him. As yet he couldn't stand, and his arm was still useless, his broken fingers unable to move. It hurt to move, it even hurt to breathe and he felt incredibly weak. The thought of travelling, even riding on a donkey, sounded overwhelmingly awful. Yet in Teon there was a joy – he had seen Gowli again, he had seen his father again. And he was to return to his land, for....He lay on his couch uncertain – his mind couldn't put together the reasons why he had to go – he had to go.

Yet Teon was willing to go. Hansa talked long to him. Hansa knew even less about what was required than Teon. She had known that she had to rescue him from the palace that night, and was lucky that they had nursed the wife of the head servant six months before through a difficult pregnancy. His wife had stayed at the commune for two months, having collapsed while passing. Everyone considered it a miracle that both wife and baby daughter survived, but both were now doing well. Hansa had been horrified at the condition Teon was in – far worse than she expected. It was a miracle he was still alive after his harsh treatment in the cells and the beatings he had received at the hands of Magrell and his men. She said over and over to Teon that he was "a chosen one", but she couldn't really tell him who had chosen him, or why, or for what.

For Teon, however, it was more than just Hansa talking of the Chosen One. He particularly remembered the voice that had said to him on two occasions – I am with you. And he had an inner conviction that he must return, had to go back for a reason. Hansa only confirmed to Teon what he knew already.

In his cell he had spent much time in despair and agony, and in that despair and agony one day had merged into another. However, something had changed when he began to notice the light, and in that light he had found the time and confidence to think. In his mind certain glimpses of events had fallen in to place. For example, that very first day, the whispered comment by Magrell. He knew for sure that Magrell had killed Hamlan. He guessed that Magrell had allowed him to escape the night the Emperor had been killed – it was too much of a coincidence that after Magrell had visited him in the cell he found the door unlocked. And he had become aware at the feast that Magrell somehow was now the Emperor. Yet so much was still missing from the story. How had he, Teon, become embroiled in the plot? How had he survived? Who were these women, these Bayronites, who had rescued him? Why had they done it? So many questions.

That night Hesteon had at last gone to sleep. Hansa was bidding Teon goodnight as well when a thought struck Teon. He put the thought into words to Hansa. "Could you leave a candle burning in this room tonight". Somehow in his cell it had been the burning lamp that had turned him around. Perhaps a light would give him the strength for the journey which, he knew, could be as bad as anything he had faced up to now. At first Hansa had refused, but Teon, with sudden strength, had said to her "You must light the candle". She looked at him for a moment, then bowed her head to him and lit the candle. With that she withdrew to her own bed.

Teon stared long and hard at the candle. Even he did not know why the candle was suddenly so important. He felt sleep taking over him, but as he did he began to see the face of a child in the light. He wasn't sure if it was a girl or boy, but he knew it was a child's face, perhaps seven or eight years old. It may have been a hallucination, a dream, his mind playing tricks, the effects of the beatings he had taken, the awful pain he still felt throughout his body and the herbs given to him by the women of the commune to try and alleviate the pain. He had even thought it might have been one of the women of the commune playing a trick on him – perhaps Hansa trying to find a way to encourage him. Deep down he knew it was something else. Someone else. The face had appeared slowly, first the eyes, then nose and mouth. It was the eyes that held Teon's gaze, eyes of great depth and great sorrow. Suddenly he saw the face moving, speaking to him. He heard the whispered voice in his head. "You must speak for me. You must say my words". The voice was the last thing he was aware of as sleep swept over him.

11

Magrell was worried: he realised that he had changed, or rather was changing. He could talk to no-one about it, but that night at the feast he realised he was different: the events of the previous three weeks had changed him. Up to that moment he had kept a clear head, and had been happy to use the tools he needed, whether blackmail, bribery, murder or violence, or anything else, for the ends he had, to fulfil his ambition to be Emperor. His plan to become Emperor had been flawless, had worked to perfection. He was more than happy to use people, any people, to achieve his ends. He knew he was in control. But that night at the feast he had realised something new – he enjoyed the violence. With hindsight the frenzy of the beating he had given to someone he knew was innocent had shocked him. Beating an innocent youth well past the point of death had left him stunned. He had enjoyed it. He also reflected that it was good so much drink had flowed, because through the drink no-one in that room would have seen the ecstasy in his face as he beat the boy unconscious, and then beyond, to death. He was aware that something deep within him had seeped into his consciousness: he enjoyed the violence, he craved the opportunity to kill again. It was a feeling he believed, was certain, he could control. He also had discovered that it was a feeling that was part of him, in a way he had never known before.

As Magrell sat in his tent at the border with Fethon, he was aware that no-one else could know, or ever should know of this blood lust. He pondered on what might happen the next day.

The seven day deadline Magrell had given Jayron ran out the next day. Magrell was planning the campaign – he was certain that Jayron would try to protect his own companions and people, that he would not give up the people on Magrell's list. Magrell knew he could sweep through the country and be in Durringham the next night, but he had other plans. Perhaps motivated by a need to show his power and contempt for his

74

neighbour, perhaps driven by this new sense of bloodlust that had come to him, he had decided to take things more slowly. The next day he would simply move his encampment over the border. He would destroy anything in his way. For twenty-four hours he would allow his soldiers to pillage other villages in the area. Then, in one swoop he would march into Durringham, sweeping aside all resistance, taking the land at will.

Magrell knew that at the moment he chose, Fethon would be in his hands. He would make the thrill of taking a new land last, both for his own enjoyment, the enjoyment of his troops and the humiliation of the Fethonites. Already Magrell was viewing this as a carnival rather than an invasion.

It was dark, the fire barely glowing, lighting the movement of the one person who was awake. Comp moved, then woke his son – called Compson – and daughter, Anga. Comp whispered in his harsh northern tongue. "Go. Food. Carry. Supplies." The other two got quickly and quietly to their feet, put on their rough sandals, then picked up packs they had prepared the night before.

The three of them left the clan and made for the rough path that headed south from their territory; Angala, unknown to them, had watched them leave as she had watched them go each morning. The path south ran close by their camping ground, and soon began to climb. The climb took about two hours, up the rocky path, then the path levelled out onto the high grasslands. The small group of north people travelled quietly and quickly but without tiring. There was still only moonlight as they crossed the high plain half running, half walking.

There was little to be seen, but the group of north people were clear where they were headed. Within a further hour they reached the tumbled-down hut, and were inside. After checking around the hut to see if there had been any visitors they opened their packs and took out the food they had been carrying. They looked over the food that was already on the table, removing any that was going off and replacing it with the food they had brought.

Comp then turned to three lamps on another table. From a flask of oil he filled each one – enough to burn over twenty-four hours. The North People checked the rugs in the hut to ensure they were still dry. None of the three spoke – they had done this every morning for almost a week now. Within minutes the three figures disappeared northwards into the darkness as silently as they had arrived.

Early in the morning Hesteon and Teon set out. Teon managed to climb off his bed by himself and stood on the floor, but quickly had to sit on a chair – his legs giving way beneath him. It took Hesteon, Hansa and the other women a few minutes to put the adapted saddle onto the donkey and to gather the few items that belonged to Hesteon and his son. Hesteon himself lifted Teon onto the donkey – Hesteon amazed how much weight Teon had lost in the weeks since they had been together in Mayeringham. Just after dawn they set out.

The route they took headed north out of Gresk along a much smaller track than the one to Fethon. The route was also much quieter, and few people passed them. The track headed north for an hour, for about three miles until it divided. Hesteon knew he had to take the left fork. Without stopping they turned west and headed towards the high plateau.

The other track – the right fork – headed towards the northern wastes where few people journeyed, where the residents, the north people, were considered to be wild and untamed. The northern wastes belonged to no-one. The tribes there were nomadic, mountain people, reputed to live in warrior groups. Few had even met the northern people. Those who had, described them as wild, unkempt, alien, unsociable, unfriendly. Even Magrell in his ambitions as yet had no ambition to conquer the north people. At the moment they kept themselves to themselves, they were no trouble to Bayron, and Bayron would gain little from them. At the moment Magrell was happy to leave the north people to themselves. Of course in the future he might invade, but at the moment there was little point, and little to be gained from such a poor people.

Hesteon and Teon talked sporadically as they journeyed north. They talked briefly of Gowli. They talked about their home back in Mayeringham. Teon even said one or two things about his own journey to Gresk and about life in the cell, talking only of the daily routine, not mentioning any of the other events surrounding his time in Gresk – too much of what had happened was still too horrific to recall. Hesteon told him what had happened at Mayeringham after Teon had left, and told him about his and Gowli's journey to Gresk, about their time in the commune. For Teon riding was difficult enough – he was more than happy to leave most of the conversation to Hesteon.

As for Hesteon, he was trying to sort a whole range of emotions in his mind. He had now accepted that Teon had not killed Hamlan or the Emperor, although a small corner of him still doubted. Hesteon was feeling the loss of his home and his best friend Gowli. The most confusing of all for Hesteon was the change in relationship with his son. Until Teon had been taken to Gresk they had been everyone's ideal picture of a Father and son relationship. Now that had all changed. Teon had suffered dreadful things alone. He had seen and experienced horrors no young person should experience. Hesteon still felt the desire to protect his son, yet Hesteon knew that things had all changed. In some ways Teon had been taken out of his hands. On one level he was still caring for Teon and helping him on the journey – a journey Teon couldn't make without his help. Yet Teon was now about someone else's business. Teon had become, in ways that Hesteon could not understand, far more important than "his son". And Teon was different. There was something in him which had never been there before. There were the blazing eyes. Teon knew nothing of his "blazing eyes", but both Hansa and Gowli had noticed them, as had Hesteon. Hesteon still cared passionately for Teon but now he almost felt himself to be Teon's servant.

As Hesteon and the donkey, with Teon riding, turned to the West the path began slowly to climb and their conversation became less. The landscape around them was very much open grassland, and occasionally they saw herds of sheep or goats being tended by young lads – many of the men had been part of the muster to form the army to invade Fethon. None of them bothered with the pair making their slow and weary progress across the grasslands.

At midday the two of them and the donkey stopped by a stream. Hesteon had to lift Teon off the Donkey and stand him on the grass. Teon was still able to stand only for a very short time before he sat, helped to the floor by Hesteon. He had found the donkey ride, despite the adapted saddle, very uncomfortable, and at times very painful – he was glad of the break. At the same time Hesteon relieved the donkey of its load, and allowed it to wander and graze and drink as it wanted. They knew that they would have to allow the donkey at least an hour to graze and recover, so after eating Teon lay on the warm grass and slept. Hesteon kept watch, although for nothing in particular. He was pleased to see Teon sleeping because he knew the journey would get much harder before it became easier.

The afternoon did indeed become much harder. The path became rockier and more windy as they continued to climb. As the grasslands turned to rocks they saw fewer and fewer signs of life. There had been one boy with about ten goats, and a small homestead about a mile off the track, then nothing through the rest of the afternoon. Hesteon knew they were heading for "the upper plateau", a high grassland that no-one inhabited and few crossed. Some were scared of the northern people who were said to journey there. Most simply put off by the total dreariness and barrenness of the plateau.

Hesteon once travelled there in his youth. He remembered that there was a rickety travellers' hut on the plateau, and he hoped to reach the hut before nightfall. However, the journey was much harder than he expected or remembered. The donkey had to rest at intervals, as did Teon. The track was at times steeper than he remembered from his younger days, and there was a constant danger of stumbling on the rocky path, occasionally a long drop to one side of the path or the other. All afternoon they struggled along the track, climbing ever higher. Too often they had to stand to catch their breath. Hesteon was also concerned that the journey was not good for Teon – sometimes he would see Teon grimace in pain, he would see him wince in discomfort; frequently Teon would break into coughing fits, but he never complained.

Once on a particularly steep section the donkey simply couldn't carry Teon, who had to dismount and walk. It was as Hesteon led the donkey up this part that he heard Teon cry out, and on rushing back found him sprawled on the ground. He had tripped on some rocks, and was lying on his side gasping for breath, unable to stand by himself. It took several minutes for Teon to recapture his breath, and even longer for Hesteon to carry him up the difficult section to the donkey.

It wasn't until dusk, well into the evening, that they felt the path level out. Hesteon had a sudden surge of relief that the climb was over. They first noticed the path easing, then the grassland beginning in the rocks, then finally they climbed over the ridge to see the grasslands of the high plateau spread out before them. In the far distance – still several miles away – through the remaining half-light they saw a small hut, the hut they hoped to make that night. The grasslands were very different from those they had crossed leaving Gresk that morning. These were bleak, damp, remote, whereas those lower down had been dry, warm, full of life. Hesteon thought these grasslands were dead, but then remembered that grass lived. He felt that here only the grass lived. The only thing to break the grass was the stone path ahead of them.

12

Hesteon called for another rest, then they began the journey to the hut. Teon insisted he try to walk as far as he could, and struggled a hundred yards before he had to remount the donkey. As they walked to the hut the darkness closed in on them, but the moon showed them the path for a few yards ahead. The night was also turning cold, the dew forming, as they walked on for what seemed an age. The cold and damp seemed to make Teon's cough even worse. He was coughing almost non-stop by this stage. Then out of the gloom, still some distance away they saw the wooden hut, looking shabby and tumbled down, but lit up by the moon. Again Teon insisted on walking, and was helped off the donkey by Hesteon, and together they shambled towards the hut ahead.

It took Hesteon and Teon a further hour to reach the hut. When they arrived, around midnight, it took them a couple of minutes to find the door on the other side of the hut from their approach. They turned the handle on the door, which had no lock, and pushed it open, but then stopped where they were. Inside the hut, framed by the door there was light. From outside it looked dark and dilapidated but now with the door open they felt something there.

Teon hobbled first into the cabin, looked around quickly but saw no-one there. He quickly took in the room. In the middle was a low round table made of stone stood on a single pedestal. On the table stood three lamps burning, giving the light they had encountered on opening the door. Along the two sides of the hut to either side of the door were benches, perhaps for sitting on or for sleeping on, covered in rugs. The greatest surprise: opposite the door, against the wall, was another table with fresh food on. There was bread, meat, fresh fruit, which had been standing there for at most a couple of days. There was a jug of water and goblets. There was no sign of people, indeed no sign that people lived there – there was no fire, no used dishes, no clothes there.

Both Hesteon and Teon felt the irony – this hut that looked so shabby on the outside was so well kept inside, and clearly someone visited regularly to provide the fresh food.

Teon felt encouraged by what they had found and beckoned for Hesteon to come into the room. Hesteon tied the donkey to a post by the door, then followed Teon into the room, his sword drawn. Both stood in silence, until Teon spoke quietly. "It is all right". He waved for Hesteon to follow him and hobbled around the stone table to the food. He began to eat and drink, managing only a little before he could take no more. Hesteon, exhausted from the day's efforts, took little persuading and also began to eat. After both had eaten what they wanted they felt they only had the energy to find the nearest place to sleep. Within minutes Hesteon lay on one of the benches and was fast asleep. Both were too exhausted to wonder who had prepared the food.

Teon had eaten well, but knew it wasn't a good day for him. As he moved to the nearest bench Teon reflected. He was walking better, just a bit better, but he was still very weak and the riding on the donkey had not helped him. If anything, his cough had become worse, particularly through the cold and damp of the evening on the high plateau. He also knew that his broken arm was not good. It still hurt and was useless, hanging heavily and limply from his shoulder. The second time it had been kicked – by Magrell in his frenzy – whatever healing had taken place was undone. This time he had no sense that the arm was improving, and this feeling was made worse by his broken fingers on the same arm. After a few moments, Teon too lay on one of the benches and wrapped the rugs around him – at least they would sleep warmly and comfortably this night. For perhaps a minute his coughing enveloped him, but he managed to get the cough under control. He looked at the lights on the table, but as he began to wonder what they might be, he fell fast asleep.

For Teon and Hesteon the night passed in deep deep sleep. If anything moved in the night, they did not hear it. Indeed, for most of the night nothing did – the upper plateau was a very lonely place to be.

They certainly didn't hear the door of the hut open in the hour before dawn, perhaps five hours after they had gone to sleep. They did not hear the strangers walking around the outside of the hut. They did not see the person stood in the doorway in silhouette formed by the moonlight. They were, however, immediately woken and roused by the horrendously shrill scream reverberating around the hut. In seconds Hesteon was on his feet grabbing his sword. Teon too tried to stand, but he simply fell to the floor, landing on his front, his good arm beneath him. Falling on his arm he had winded himself again, and he found moving at all painful to his chest. While Hesteon moved to defend them, for Teon there was only the horror of falling on the floor and the pain, both new pain and old which took over his body in that moment.

Hesteon's eyes were turned to the door, transfixed by the wild warrior people – three of whom were now framed by the door. Hesteon would fight – but fear told him they would not survive.

13

Magrell woke that morning in buoyant mood. Today would be the first day not just of his victory over Fethon, but of his humiliation of Jayron. He breakfasted with Haren, the wife he had married to achieve all he had. Haren was still widely respected in the nation but Magrell had nothing but contempt for her. Having an affair with the king's cousin Ganerr, then giving in to a simple piece of blackmail without even thinking if there were other options – it had left him with nothing but contempt for her.

Magrell had also ordered Ganerr to the front, and Ganerr dined in the tent next to theirs. Magrell had already organised the end of Ganerr. Magrell also took the opportunity to humiliate Haren. He spoke to her jovially. "Darling", the sarcasm oozed from his voice. "Darling, this day you will see me achieve what your husband never had the guts to do, or should I say your former husband. Today you see the beginning of the building of MY Bayronite empire." His voice emphasised the word "My". Haren said nothing. Her spirits were low from the humiliation of her affair being found out; from being forced to marry this cold man. She despised herself for allowing him to use her to become Emperor. She was also certain it would only be a matter of time before she too would be dead. It would only take Magrell a short time to become the common man's hero and he would need her no more. He simply had to produce the letter that he kept revealing her affair. It would give him all the grounds he would need for her execution.

Magrell knew that the inhabitants had fled the villages over the border, and he had confirmed this by sending patrols the evening before. He felt he should be, at least symbolically, the first person to step over the border. However, for Magrell it was more than symbolism, he had another reason to go to the village opposite. He wanted to revisit the beginning of all that had happened over these past four weeks. He recognised Mayeringham as the place where Hamran, the Emperor's son, had met his death. Somehow, in his joy, he felt that he had to give thanks, or pay tribute, or at least mark the spot where his ambition had begun to be fulfilled.

By mid morning the Bayronite troops were drawn up in parade. Magrell left his camp, walked across the front of his troops waving to them, then walked towards the Mayeringham. A line of posts marked the border, but no-one was there to defend. As he reached one of the border cairns, Magrell stopped, then turned to the soldiers who gathered to watch him. He bowed to them, then stepped into Fethon. A great cheer arose from the ranks behind him as Magrell began to take Fethon unopposed. Magrell walked to the edge of the village fifty yards away. Again he stopped, turned and bowed to his followers, and the great cheer rose into the sky once more.

Magrell turned to see an old man stood in front of him. The old man spoke "You will not pass". Magrell recognised the coward who had been the village elder only weeks before. The pathetic leader who had been happy to sacrifice a youngster for his own safety. He recognised the man, although he had forgotten the name Bohran.

Bohran spent the time in his hut after the villagers had fled. He would not go. He spent the time in despair and confusion, such that he had little idea what he was doing. The evening before he had been lying in his bedchamber when some soldiers had broken into his house. They had sat, drinking Bohran's beer while Bohran lay in bed in the next room listening to them. The men were in celebratory mood, and the ale loosened their tongues. He heard enough. He knew Magrell was to enter the village alone in the morning as a grand gesture. He knew the soldiers were to follow at midday. He knew they were to camp outside the village after having torched the houses. He knew enough and knew he had to take a stand, as futile as it might be. For Bohran he felt there was one noble effort left in him. Now he stood face to face with Magrell, determined that Magrell should not pass. Bohran in his confusion saw it as the one thing he had to do. In his confusion he did not recognise the futility of what he had chosen to do, only the duty which was his. He spoke again: "You will not pass".

Magrell stopped and looked at the old man who stood before him unarmed. He saw the blank look in the man's eyes and heard the voice challenging him to stop. Bohran spoke again, repeating the formula all elders in Fethon knew. "By the power given to me as village elder in the land of Fethon, you will not pass."

Magrell stood looking at the crazed old man. His thoughts ranged. He wondered how his patrols had not found this man yesterday – someone would pay dearly for that mistake. He wondered how this man had found the courage to make this stand. He wondered if there was help here for himself. He felt contempt for the coward opposite. Inside he laughed at the utter futility of the old man's stand. The one thing Magrell did not feel was fear. He was a man fit and armed. He faced an old man, unarmed and crazed.

"I will pass," said Magrell pulling his sword from its sheath. In one moment he had leapt forward and caught the old man across the side of his head with the flat side of his sword. Instantly the old man crumpled into an unconscious heap. Magrell pulled a sheet of paper from his pocket and quickly put it into the tunic of the elder lying stunned on the floor. He knew this would be more convincing. He then walked back to the border and called his guards. He gave them instructions to bring the man to the front of his tent after his evening meal. Magrell returned to his tent and gave the order for the encampment to be moved into Fethon.

All that day the army moved its encampment into Fethon, setting up camp a mile over the border beyond the village. Different groups were detailed for different tasks. Early in the afternoon the village of Mayeringham was first looted, as little as there was to be taken, then torched. The smoke drifted northwards, as the flames leapt high into the sky. By evening there was little left of the village. Other patrols were sent out to other villages – all now well deserted – to forage for food and supplies.

By evening the Bayronite camp was set up, and Magrell was ready to dine. That evening he dined with Haren and Ganerr, outside his tent – Haren was surprised Ganerr was invited. Little was said, though Magrell appeared to enjoy the meal enormously. When the meal was finished he called for the old man to be brought to him, and for his elite guard to remain, along with some of his generals.

Magrell turned to the soldiers who were guarding the old man and gave the order: "Bring him here." The old man was still dazed from his earlier blow as he stood before Magrell, his hands tied behind his back.

Magrell spoke directly to the guards. "Have you searched this man? Have you discovered anything from your interrogation of him?" The guards remained silent for a moment, then the Sergeant stepped forward.

"Sir", he said in a formal military voice. "We have interrogated the man but he had nothing to say. However, sir, we found this letter on the man." The soldier handed over to Magrell an envelope.

Magrell took the envelope and began to open it. He tore the top, then begun to draw a sheet of paper out of the envelope. No-one was looking at Ganerr, but if they had they would have seen him grip the arms of his chair and turn deathly pale.

Magrell opened the paper slowly and dramatically. He looked at the paper as if he had never seen it before. He looked as if he were reading it. Finally he looked up, held the paper up, turned it around several times and asked quietly: "Does anyone recognise this?"

There were no voices, just puzzled expressions. For moments there was silence, then Magrell turned sharply on his heel to look straight at Ganerr. He pointed at Ganerr and repeated his question sharply. "Do you recognise this?"

Ganerr began to sweat icily and to stammer. How had this got on the man? How had this got into the hands of Magrell? How had this appeared here? How did the old man have it? Ganerr recognised a sheet of paper torn from his personal diary. The sheet, he knew, described the Bayronites plan of attack and kept a record of Magrell's activities. He was suddenly aware of the folly of keeping a diary, the folly of thinking he could keep it and then publish his diary of the glory of Bayronite victory. He hoped that publishing his diaries would line his pockets and finance more drinking. The folly of thinking he could clear his debts and make his fortune by publishing his record of the events of this time. He had no idea how the sheet of paper had appeared from the old man's pocket – he thought no-one knew of the diary.

Inwardly Magrell smiled, thinking the gods had smiled on him. Or thinking that things were at least going his way. He had received the letter only the day before from one of Ganerr's servants, a servant who thought he could make himself some money from serving the Emperor. Magrell had accepted the envelope, but the servant made nothing – he was never seen again. It was a small step from receiving the envelope and meeting the old man to creating the circumstances to end Ganerr's ambition – and life – forever.

Magrell continued. "We find details of our plan of attack, our forces, our plans for after the invasion all written in the hand of Ganerr. We find this record on one of the leaders of our enemy. Gentlemen, there is only one conclusion we can draw."

The voices of the soldiers began to jeer at Ganerr. Voices shouted traitor at him. Voices accused him of spying. Swords were waved at him. Soldiers pressed in around him. For several minutes this went on until Magrell raised his hand. The noise quickly abated.

When there was silence, Magrell pointed at Bohran who still stood there in a daze. He gave orders curtly. Turning to the guard he said: "take him out and make sure that he does not see the darkness come." Two soldiers stepped forward and took Bohran by the arms, leading him, still looking dazed, back towards Mayeringham. Magrell turned to the Sergeant. "Sergeant. Bring two of your most trusted soldiers. It is my responsibility to see that this traitor does no more damage."

Haren watched the sergeant, the two soldiers and Magrell, along with Ganerr, now with hands tied behind his back, heading towards the woods to the south of the village. She knew she would never see Ganerr alive again.

14

After lying on the floor for several minutes, Teon struggled onto his side his eyes clenched shut in pain, his cough returning with a vengeance. He felt his chest hurting horribly as he coughed but he guessed wrongly the newly broken ribs were just bruising from where his weight had landed on his arm. The small part of his mind not fighting the pain thought ruefully – just one more part of his body that would hurt, one more part that was broken.

Teon heard the sound of voices. He forced his eyes open and looked up. He saw, two figures peering down at him from less than two feet away. When they saw Teon fall they had both ignored Hesteon and rushed to where the boy was slumped on the floor. Hesteon moved towards them threateningly with his staff, so the third person simply grabbed the staff from his hand, broke it in half and threw Hesteon to the ground. He took a short sword from under his cloak, knelt on Hesteon's chest and held the sword to Hesteon's neck, almost daring Hesteon to move, to try to fight back.

Teon felt panic rising in him, although he could not move to act on it. It took him three or four minutes to get the panic under control and look more carefully around himself. Teon noticed that the two looking down at him both had untidy, wild, black hair. Both wore coarse tunics and trousers made of a rough brown cloth, both had dark skin, but the two figures were very different. One was a man, with beard matching his hair. He was strong, muscular, and had bright lively eyes. The man stood over 6 feet tall. Beside him, but perhaps a foot shorter, stood a girl, maybe the same age as Teon. She too had the wild glint in her eyes, but seemed much more nervous than the man.

The two figures were talking animatedly to each other, and to a third of their number whom Teon could not see, in a language that puzzled him – a language that seemed half familiar, a language he could not understand but felt he should. Teon was certain these were the north people. Surprisingly, having looked at the strangers, he felt no fear – perhaps he had no fear left to feel.

The two people stopped talking to each other when they saw Teon open his eyes: they stood still, simply watching him from two feet away. Teon struggled painfully into a sitting position, then looked slowly around the room again. His eyes moved, and turned to see Hesteon lying on the ground, the third of the northmen sitting on him holding a sword to his throat. Hesteon looked terrified. Teon turned to the two stood in front of him and whispered with all the voice he could muster. "Please let him go."

For a moment no-one moved, then the taller of the two signalled to his companion. Immediately the northman removed his sword from Hesteon's neck and stood to his feet. Teon noticed that the companion was younger, perhaps in his early twenties, although he had the same hair and beard and clothes as the older man.

Teon turned again to the two stood in front of him. He was surprised to see that the whole room – his father, the three north people – seemed to be waiting on him. After what seemed an eternity, the girl suddenly pointed at him. He turned and examined her properly for the first time. The tears on her face were the last thing he expected to see. She peered at him, and then in reverence spoke two words. "Him. Chosen". Teon recognised the voice – the same as had screamed out only minutes before.

The girl had broken the ice of silence and her father quickly stood upright. He busied himself, taking food from his bag and placing it on the table opposite the door. He returned to Hesteon, now sitting on the floor and Teon still lying. He pointed, this time towards the food on the table. He spoke in a deep, surprisingly warm, voice. "Friends. Eat."

At that moment the atmosphere in the room relaxed. Hesteon rose to his feet, and with the older man pointing to the food, he and the two north men moved towards it, suddenly aware of their hunger. The girl stayed beside Teon who was still sitting weakly on the floor. The relaxation of the moment had a different effect on Teon as he was suddenly doubled up again with coughing, a hack that seemed to fill his body, that shook him from head to toe. Jagging pain seared through Teon, the cough hurting his chest where he had fallen in a way that it had not before. Teon knew that his coughing was getting worse again after improving while he had been at the commune. Now the pain was far worse, compounded as it was by the blow to his ribs.

The coughing fit seemed to sap all the energy Teon had, but as it subsided he tried to rise to his feet. His legs gave way before he was halfway to upright. He sat down hard on one of the benches. The girl sat beside him and put her arms around his shoulders to steady him. The other three gathered around him, concerned. The girl looked at the younger of the two men and spoke. "Food. Drink." Quickly the younger man stepped away and was back in moments.

Teon drank slowly from the goblet of water offered to him by the younger man, then took a few bites at the fruit offered to him before pushing the other food away.

The older of the men, obviously the leader of the group, spoke again. "Not travel now. Later. Boy bad." He spoke in a voice that no-one could disagree with.

Again, silence until Hesteon spoke. "Who are you?"

The older man pointed towards one of the walls of the hut, "people of north".

"But you speak as we do."

The old man paused. "We tell story. Time we have."

"Long past, Northmen refugees. Fethon chase us. Send us to mountains. We thrive. New life made. We see face. We People of North". Teon and Hesteon struggled to make sense of the words. Their languages had a common root, but the Northern version had obviously taken its own path over the years.

It was Teon who asked the next question. "But here..."

The older man spoke again. "Continue. We serve face. Wait for you. Want face for all men. We hear. Chosen one coming. Face send message. Angala hear. Hansa send you. Meet chosen one. At Golo. We prepare. Golo ready. We come. Dawn. Today. Chosen one." He pointed at Teon.

Hesteon had been listening hard and had been taken aback half way through. "Hansa?" he asked.

The Older man looked at him. "She North. She see face".

Still something else bothered Hesteon. "The scream" – he pointed to the girl, "You screamed".

The girl suddenly smiled, a smile so unexpected it lit up the room. She also looked slightly sheepish. She spoke for the first time. "Not see Donkey. It kick. Stupid donkey". As she spoke she lifted the left leg of her trousers. Down the shin was a deep graze six inches long where the Donkey's foot had caught her. "Sting", she said, ruefully. Hesteon and the two north men laughed. Teon also began to laugh, but the pain in his chest was excruciating. His laugh stopped just as quickly, to be replaced by coughing.

By now all sorts of questions were crowding into Hesteon's mind. "You mentioned a name. You mentioned Golo, or something like that."

The older man spoke again. "This place Golo. Centre. Face ride. To world. Here."

Hesteon and the North people fell silent, their conversation ended for the moment. After many minutes it was Teon who had broken the silence in his whisper. "I must continue my journey to Fethon. We will start at midday. I will be strong enough". The silence returned to the room as they all sat with their own thoughts.

Again it was Teon who broke the silence. He whispered. "I, too, have seen the face".

Durringham, Jayron's capital, was full of people. Many of them were refugees. Others were traders taking shelter from the coming onslaught, hoping against hope to escape the invading armies. Jayron, surveying his city, knew that if there was fighting, the people of the city would be very vulnerable. He knew that if he tried to defend Durringham defeat might be delayed, but in the end the slaughter by the Bayronites would be too awful to contemplate. He knew he could only save these people if he chose a different path, but what path?

Jayron sent messengers to the Bayronite army – he had made his decision. He believed he only had one choice. Three miles north of Durringham was an area of flat land, perfect flat ground in a circular amphitheatre, a hundred and fifty yards diameter. Some said it was natural, others said it was man-made.

It was an area of land that the Fethonites held sacred, and was the place where the Fethonite kings were always crowned. It was also the place where the annual assembly of the people met, where the king went to meet with anyone who had a complaint or suggestion or need, an assembly that often lasted four weeks. The area was called simply the throne of Fethon, or the Throneland.

The Throneland was particularly special for Jayron. It was an area where he had met the people, and where the people had met a just and good king. It was here in his dealings with his people that they had seen something of the great king he would become. For Jayron, the throne of Fethon represented what he as king stood for – to unite, support, challenge and serve his people.

Jayron's messengers gave Magrell the invitation from Jayron: for him and his army to meet him at the throne of Fethon, at a time suitable to Magrell. Magrell, considering Jayron's possible motives, could see only one possible reason for the invitation – Jayron wanted to surrender, and in surrendering save his people. Magrell was happy to accept the surrender, but it would not stop the slaughter – the people of Fethon would have no potential rebels when he had finished, no potential warriors. Bayron would rule, and Bayron would receive full tribute from the country.

It was early in the morning when the messengers from Jayron arrived. Magrell greeted them and heard what they had to say. He informed them that he would come, but at a time of his choosing, then he sent them on their way.

For Magrell, the carnival atmosphere of the campaign was growing and growing. It started the day before they had moved their camp into Fethon. Now, in his urge to further humiliate Jayron he had agreed to accept his surrender, but he would not go today. This day would be a day of celebration. He would have competitions for his warriors. Races. Jousting. Wrestling. He would get his catering section to organise a big feast for the afternoon from food taken from villages in the area. They would celebrate this day; they would carnival this day; then on the morrow march and take Fethon.

Only one thing was causing some concern to Magrell, and this was something deeply personal. He felt his blood lust growing stronger. It had happened the night before when he and the small group of soldiers had taken Ganerr into the woodland, and he was remembering the events then. It hadn't been enough to simply kill him. He had tortured him, allowed him to scream out, allowed him to beg for mercy, and in the end sat there transfixed as the mans blood and life ebbed away. He had sent the guards back to the camp after they had tied Ganerr to a tree then allowed Ganerr to suffer for at least half an hour before death had come. He left the woodland elated beyond anything he had ever known before. Something deep within him had been satisfied by his control over this man's life and death. Magrell was concerned that this lust should not affect his judgements which until now had been sharp.

Magrell pushed the worries to the back of his mind: the day went as Magrell hoped. The day was a great celebration. The soldiers partied, and competed, and drank freely. The feast was as good as they had hoped – so much had been left behind by the Fethonites in their rush to safety. So much was sitting there to be taken. The celebration went well, the troops were happy, and for Magrell there was no cloud on the horizon. Tomorrow he would not just be Emperor of Bayron, but Fethon would be his as well.

At midday the five people in the hut ate more of the food, then made ready to journey. The two men of the north put packs on their backs and picked up their staffs. The girl too was readying herself for the journey by packing some of the fruit. All but Teon were bustling around, loading the Donkey, gathering food and blankets. It was as they were about to leave that Teon spoke.

"Wait". His voice was quiet, but demanded attention. "We must talk further". The other four looked at each other, then gathered around him.

"I'm sorry" continued Teon looking to the three north people, "I do not even know your names".

The older man introduced the three: he was called Comp. The younger man called Compson. The girl was called Anga. It was only now that Hesteon and Teon realised this was father, son and daughter.

Teon continued to speak in the chesty whisper that had become his voice. "Comp", he said, "I cannot fight, but I must return to my people. If I cannot fight then there is no point in taking warriors with me." He looked directly at the three north people. "You cannot travel where I travel. You must return home."

All three were taken aback, but somehow Teon was not to be argued with. All stood in silence for many seconds. Hesteon and the three north people felt out of their depth: Teon made no sense in his certainty. It was Anga who spoke into the silence. "We not go, we not go home." Her face broke again, illuminating the hut with her smile.

Teon again spoke insistently. "You cannot go with me. I must travel alone. Too many of us may cause us problems. We might be spotted. You look different. We would arouse too much suspicion."

It was Anga who again defied him. "Father, brother, here wait. Nurse Teon need. Anga Nurse. Anga go."

Teon had no energy left to argue, and besides, Anga had tended him through the morning and he knew she spoke truly – she was a good nurse. After a brief pause Teon nodded in agreement and let Comp lift him carefully onto the donkey. Teon did not look back as Hesteon, Anga and he, sat on the donkey, set off along the track towards Fethon.

For the first part of this journey they would go further across the high plateau, but then towards evening they would descend through the rocky lands into Fethon. They knew the path came into the north of the land, but there would still be many miles to Durringham. Comp and Compson watched them go, as confused as many others who had met Teon.

The first part of the journey for the small group was eventless as they travelled through the characterless and damp upper plateau. Occasionally a frog would be disturbed, or perhaps a shrew; sometimes some sort of hawk would fly across their path, but otherwise nothing moved in this land. Teon realised that somehow Anga was taking more and more care of him, holding his arm as he rode the donkey, while Hesteon held the rope to the donkey's head and led the way. They stopped occasionally for a rest, and once Teon inspected his chest where he had fallen on his arm earlier and saw a bruise six inches across developing purple and blue against his white skin. By now he was also hearing the occasional click of bone from his chest and had guessed it was more than bruising, a view that was confirmed by the jagging pain he regularly felt. He also knew there was little to be done for broken ribs except hurt! And then give them time to heal, time he didn't have. The sun was sinking in the West as they reached the ridge around the edge of the plateau and saw their route down into Fethon, following a rocky gully. As they sat on the ridge looking down its rocky face, the path looked terrifying, but in both Hesteon and Teon there was a lifting of their spirits. It was the path that would take them to their homeland. Whatever was left of their homeland.

Magrell lay in his tent, content with the day. His greatest enemy from his homeland – Ganerr – was now gone. Amongst his soldiers he was popular, and if you have the loyalty of the soldier you have the loyalty of the nation. There may have been dissenting voices on the council, but his popularity and strength would keep them quiet until he could get rid of them.

Magrell was also content because he had learnt over the previous weeks the strength that he possessed. The strength to blackmail and control the former Emperor's wife. The strength to kill the Emperor and his son. The strength to see off his enemies. The strength to draw loyalty out of others. Magrell had found a confidence in himself and in his strength that he knew would carry him to greater and greater triumphs, greater and greater power. He even dared to imagine himself ruler of the known world, invincible, Magrell the Mighty, but that was for the future – now he still had Fethon to capture and dominate.

Magrell lay on his bunk thinking through the next day. How he would use the events at the throne of Fethon. How he would humiliate the king. How he would control the people with a mixture of stick and carrot, violence and reward, fear and favour. He organised his plan in his mind. Tomorrow the humiliating of Jayron, the next day the destruction of Durringham.

As he dozed and his mind travelled to the destruction of Durringham, his mind began to picture the death, the carnage that would surely take place. His mind travelled to the boy he had brutally kicked to death. He mind travelled to the torture and death of Ganerr. His mind felt the sword piercing Hamlan and the Emperor. As his mind wandered, so the excitement in his body rose.

Magrell started awake, his pulse beating, his heart racing, his flesh sweating. His eyes turned to a frown as he realised the blood lust seemed to becoming stronger and stronger, seemed to be taking him over.

For Jayron, the day had been anything but joyful. Simply being seen as confident and strong at all times was tiring of itself in the face of his own despair. But there was so much more to be done. He journeyed to the throne of Fethon with his household guard early in the morning, and they set up camp outside the amphitheatre. By late morning their camp was set, and there was nothing to do except wait for Magrell.

The people of Durringham watched Jayron ride out, and through the day despair increasingly settled over the town, a despair that led to paralysis. Many had great faith in Jayron, realised the greatness of the man, but few believed now there was any salvation, few believed that even Jayron could make things right, could save them.

All day in Durringham people were on the streets, standing on corners, sitting on benches talking. It was ideal ground for rumours. Many talked openly about the massacres that Magrell was planning. Some believed that there were armies coming to save them from the West. Few really had any hope, and despair was slowly taking over. Even the children seemed to lose the will and enthusiasm for play. A dark cloud had overtaken the city. No-one had the will to think hopefully. The paralysis of fear was overwhelming.

By late afternoon Jayron knew that Magrell would not come that day. He had been told about the games Magrell was holding, the party up on the border. He knew Magrell was simply using time to drain away the morale of the Fethonites. Using time to wound the soul before he destroyed the land. Jayron hoped against hope that his meeting with Magrell would produce good results for his people even if it cost him, Jayron, his life. Deep down he knew even that was a forlorn hope.

By late evening the guards were either sitting around fires, or trying to sleep. Jayron spent the evening walking from fire to fire talking to his men, encouraging them as best he could. At the same time he answered questions honestly: he could not lie to the men and tell them how good things would be, how they would be saved. He didn't believe that himself, and his men would not have believed him either. They would not serve a king who lied to them. When asked about the future he would simply answer "I don't know", the voice not of hopelessness but simply factual – he didn't know.

When it was nearly dark Jayron retreated to his own tent, lit by a single candle. For long minutes, stretching to an hour he sat in the dark, the candle his only comfort. He knew he should sleep but he felt no tiredness, no desire to sleep.

It was as he sat there he became aware of the movement of the candle, flickering back and fore. He thought there must be a strong draught in the room, but felt nothing himself, and could sense no wind outside. His eyes were drawn to the candle and he watched the movement, till suddenly he thought he saw eyes in the flames. Then he was sure, as he saw the face of a child: whether of a boy of girl he did not know. He concentrated hard and saw the sadness of the child's face, tears on the child's cheeks, as the face flickered in the candle. And then he heard the voice. Not from the candle but in his head.

The voice spoke quietly to him. "The chosen one is coming. The chosen one is coming to save."

He heard the voice say this three or four times. He had no idea who was speaking, he had no idea if the voice was related to the face in the candle. He didn't even know if the face, or for that matter the voice, were real, but in the voice and the face he found some strength. He found some comfort. In his renewed strength and comfort he fell asleep as he sat in the chair.

After sitting for a few minutes staring down into Fethon, Hesteon, Anga and Teon knew they should move on. They needed to give themselves the time to descend the rocky hillside before it was too dark to travel. For Hesteon and Teon their early elation at returning to their own land quickly dissipated and a gloom at what they might find overtook them. They knew they had to follow the path down the rocky gully that stretched before them. All were reluctant to travel for different reasons. Hesteon was sure there would be trouble, that there might be war in the land. Anga dreaded the journey to a foreign land, travelling amongst people she had never seen before, people who had probably never seen a north person before. She dreaded travelling further and further from her beloved wilderness and family in the north. For Teon the problem was much more practical. He was still in great pain. The pain in his chest felt worse and not better through the day, as the bruising covered most of his chest. He still had no use in his arm. He still found walking so difficult. His cough had lost nothing of its power to consume his body for minutes on end. Through the last two days he had come to loathe riding on the donkey. The donkey was a good animal, but the riding seemed to shake him to the centre of his being. At times he thought his skeleton was going to fall to pieces. At the thought of his skeleton falling to pieces he smiled – it was so absurd, and he found the strength to get to his feet and began walking down the rock path very carefully.

Teon could only stagger down the path for a few minutes, holding on to the donkey or to Anga; at times when the path was wide enough, holding on to both. Soon Hesteon lifted him back onto the donkey and he rode again.

As they journeyed – Anga by his side, Hesteon ahead leading the donkey – Teon found Anga quite talkative in her own north people's way. He heard how the north people followed the face; he heard how they lived in clans – small groups of seven or eight families; how they used tents and travelled with livestock. He heard about Comp being the leader of their clan, and Compson being silent, but a great, fearless and strong hunter. She also spoke of her mother, Angala, the mother of the clan who had so much compassion, so much wisdom. Angala who had so much to do to help the families survive in their harsh environment. This was why she had not been with them at the hut that the north people called Golo. She also talked of Hansa, how she had a great vision that the three peoples of the known world could be brought together, how the Bayronite, Fethonite and north people could be united, but only united in service of the face, the vision that had appeared to so many. She told how she, Anga, had never met Hansa who had left before Anga was born. Anga, however, told of Hansa's reputation and the legends of her life amongst the northern peoples. She told how Hansa had travelled to Gresk and had set up the commune of women to serve the people of Gresk, and how a small group of women from the city had joined her.

Teon, as he expected, found Anga a caring nurse, despite her youth. He was also finding her a reassuring presence, holding his hand, occasionally stroking his arm if he winced in pain. He had already developed an affection for this young woman who in her quietness had such a liveliness, such a vibrancy. Even in the day he had shared with her, he had developed a great respect for the north people. He had the feeling that they, despite the wildness of their appearance, despite their reputation for barbarity, were a far greater people than either the Bayronites or the Fethonites.

The path continued into the gully, and in the shade they felt cold – particularly Teon who was sitting still on the donkey. Often the coldness brought on a coughing fit, and they had to stop frequently to allow him to recover. Once the donkey stumbled and Teon felt himself falling off, but Anga caught him, steadied him, although it caused him to scream out in pain as she grabbed his broken arm. Despite all these things they continued to make slow progress down the gully, resting regularly, until at last, towards then end of the evening they saw the gully begin to widen and the land flatten out before them.

As they saw the grasslands ahead, the path came to a stream, and instead of crossing straight over it, turned right along the bank, the path going upstream. The stream had been too deep to cross where the path joined it, but twenty yards along the water was shallower and the path forded the stream. It would be easy for the donkey to walk through, and at the same time the water raced through boulders that would easily act as stepping stones for the three people.

When they approached the crossing point their concentration wandered – the worst of the scramble down the face of the hill was over. Over this stream and they were in the grass lands once again. Over the border into Fethon. That they were "home" gave Hesteon almost a sense of elation: for him home and family were more important than anything. In the sense of elation and in the dusk, Hesteon was not properly concentrating on the path, his eyes looking longingly into his homeland.

Suddenly he was over the edge. He slipped. He fell. He landed on the rocks six feet below, the rocks beside the stream. The others heard him cry out in pain as he landed on the small rock shelf overhanging the stream. Luckily, Hesteon had released the reins of the donkey as he fell.

Anga quickly helped Teon off the donkey and set him on the grass by the track, then scrambled down to where Hesteon had landed. Hesteon sat on the rock muttering to himself. "So stupid. How could I be so stupid? So stupid." It was clear he had either badly sprained or broken an ankle.

After moments of thought, Anga began to search around for sticks strong enough to act as splints, for one that would work as a crutch. Alongside the stream were a number of low trees, thorn, birch and rowan. Within a few minutes she found some shorter branches she could use as splints, and quickly strapped Hesteon's ankle using cloth from her cloak. She broke a longer piece from one of the silver birches, trimmed off the leaves with a short knife she carried, leaving a straight stick with a v-shape at the top. She brought it to Hesteon as a crutch. Anga knew that staying here was not good – Hesteon and Teon would not cope well with the cold and damp of the night. Teon probably wouldn't survive. She helped Hesteon to his feet, helped him along the rock shelf until he could half hop, half step with the aid of his crutch and a lot of swearing to the other bank of the stream over the boulders. She returned and helped Teon over the stream, then led the donkey through the water to the other side.

After they gathered on the other side of the stream, on the path over the grasslands, they talked briefly about what was happening, what they should do. Hesteon had been this way many years before and knew there should be a settlement only a mile away. Peering through the gloom they could make out what may have been the settlement. They could make out what may have been smoke rising from a house. They had no choice: if they reached the settlement they could find hospitality, they could find help.

15

It was a strange and subdued little group who, an hour and a half later, in the dark, hobbled into the settlement. It had taken them that long to make the mile, with Hesteon and Teon alternating on the donkey, Anga leading, supporting and lifting the two men as they needed. By the time they reached the settlement it was completely dark, and only the light of a partial moon helped keep them on the track.

They headed towards the first of the houses and knocked hard on the door. There was no answer, so they moved to the next house, larger than the first. Again they knocked. They heard nothing, so knocked again. The second time they knocked they heard noises within. They heard people moving, speaking, clearly woken by the travellers. The tone of the voices inside suggested the people were very frightened by the late visitors. The small group stood and waited, then Anga knocked on the door again.

After two or three minutes a man's voice called out from behind the door. "Who is it?" The voice was laden with fear – these were dangerous times in Fethon, even on these distant outskirts of the country.

Hesteon answered. "We are travellers. We have injured people. Please help".

The voice called back. "How many of you are there?"

Hesteon replied. "Two men, one woman".

They heard a woman's fearful voice in the building. "Don't let them in. It could be a trick." Other voices joined in the discussion. There was a confusion of voices inside debating what they should do.

Hesteon knocked again on the door with his crutch and called out again. "Please help us."

Inside they heard the voices go quiet, then again both male and female began to debate even more urgently, arguing, discussing what they should do, whether to let them in. The three outside the door lost track of the debate in the confusion of voices. At last the door opened and an older man stood in the doorway holding a sword. He had been a tall and muscular man in his day, but was now slightly stooped. He would still be a considerable enemy. Behind him they glimpsed a number of other people, some of them holding swords. They guessed that this was the father and they assumed that the others were his sons and daughters and their families. They guessed right – the families had moved into the house from other parts of the settlement because of the recent events and threats to the country.

When he saw the travellers in the light of the door a mixture of puzzlement and compassion crossed the older man's face. In the darkness, dissipated a little by the house lights, he saw an older man, perhaps his own age, leaning on a stick, holding a leg off the ground. He was clearly in pain. Sat on the floor against the door frame was a younger man – perhaps only a boy. He had never seen anyone look in such a bad way as the boy did – it was an impression made worse as Teon began with another coughing fit – the cold night and the inactivity getting to him. Strangest of all was the third of the group, a young woman he guessed, but one who kept her cloak, made of brown coarse cloth, pulled well over her head hiding much of her face. The man's confusion grew as he looked: he could not understand what this group was, but of one thing he was certain, they were not Bayronites. They should receive his hospitality.

The older man signalled to his family and they came to help. One took the donkey and led it away into a different part of the settlement. Two others came to help Hesteon hobble into the house. Two others bent to help Teon, but Anga spoke sharply to them. "Care!".

They understood what she meant, but her voice sounded strange. They carefully lifted Teon, carried him into the house and lay him on rugs by the fire. As they saw the small party in the light of the room the family were even more confused. The small group seemed even stranger in the light than they did in the darkness of night. And questions came to each of the family. What were a man with a broken ankle, a girl from an alien people and an emaciated boy, doing walking into their settlement late at night? Who was the alien – she looked so different from the Fethonite and Bayronite people with her dark skin and rough voice? How had the boy got into this condition – so badly injured he was barely conscious? Most eyes were on the boy, his head covered with long hair, long whispy beard and moustache. At first sight he looked like a pair of eyes in a handful of straw. Where were they from? Why had they come? Where were they travelling?

It was not time to voice the questions now. They must minister to the travellers. The family spent several minutes resetting the splints on Hesteon's ankle which was clearly broken. They learnt from him that he had fallen on the path further up towards the high plateau. Again the questions came to them: what were they doing on the high plateau? Why had they travelled over the plateau where few dared go? But still, questions were for later: they brought food, and Hesteon and Anga ate.

Of most concern was the young lad. The warmth of the fire had eased his coughing fit. They saw him thin, injured, barely able to move. The way his hair looked suggested he had been like this for some time. Or at least suggested that many of his injuries had been caused some time ago but had not been allowed to heal. They could see that his arm would not move at all, hanging uselessly from his shoulder. His fingers were heavily but roughly bandaged, the bones probably shattered. His hair was uncombed and unkempt. His face had grown long stubble – the scruffy growth of a teenager who had not shaved for weeks. What was not covered in hair was yellow and blue from bruising.

The older man who had opened the door earlier, clearly head of the family, came and looked into Hesteon's face, thinking that, as the man and as the person who had spoken outside the door, he would be the leader of the group. He spoke gently. "My friend, I am Mayrog, head of this house. This..." he pointed to an older lady, "is Rayda my wife. These others are my sons, daughters and their families. I will introduce them properly later. We will help you all we can, you must stay here until your strength recovers, until you can travel on, if that is what you plan to do."

The older man stood to his feet, and felt he should say something to the younger lad. He walked over to him, crouched before him and looked into Teon's face. He was suddenly aware that from the young man's face, eyes were looking back at him, right into him, eyes with a fire so fierce Mayrog desperately wanted to look away, but couldn't. He had never seen eyes like this young man had. Then the lad spoke with a weakness so different from the fire in the eyes, in a throaty whisper of a voice. "We travel on tomorrow".

Mayrog felt so unsure of himself – those eyes had unsettled him. He spoke non-commitally. "We'll see", he said. Mayrog turned to the older woman in the room and gestured to Teon. "Do what you can, he needs all the help he can get". Rayda began to wash his face, then helped Teon remove some of his clothes. As she did so a number of tired but excited children entered the room from a door to one side, woken by the noise from the main room of the house, not wanting to miss what might be happening.

Rayda turned sharply to the children and snapped at them. "Be quiet!" The children immediately became quiet as she whispered to Teon "The grandchildren. So noisy. Such a nuisance. But I love them all." Rayda smiled warmly at them, then returned to Teon, taking many minutes to bandage or re-bandage his wounds, although she could do nothing for the bruising. Rayda marvelled that this lad had lived. The children, briefly, sat around Rayda and Teon watching intently how Rayda dealt with him. The next moment they moved in front of Anga staring, transfixed – they had never seen a person like this before. Suddenly after a few moments of the children's staring, Anga stuck out her tongue at them, then smiled broadly. The children giggled, and settled themselves around the room to watch what was happening.

Mayrog stood up and came to sit opposite Anga at the table. He had so many questions he wanted to ask. He began to give voice to one or two of them out. "Who are you? Where are you from? Why were you on the plateau?" He stopped as the girl raised her hand. She was only a slip of a girl, perhaps only fourteen or fifteen, but in her he recognised the same sort of strength as he had seen in the boy who now lay on the rugs in front of the fire.

The girl spoke in her strange accent. "Anga. Me. Them no names. Speak nothing." Anga was worried that Mayrog would recognise the names of the other two should she say them. She was sure that everyone in Fethon would have heard of them. Teon would have developed a notoriety in his own country.

At least Mayrog knew her name, but felt as host he deserved more. He spoke again. "Anga, we are helping you. How do we know we are not helping spies, or enemies? How do we know you are alone? Perhaps you have warriors following. Perhaps you are leading the Bayronite army here. You are strange to us. We must know. We have a right to know."

Anga thought for a moment and knew he was right. She spoke again. "All not tell. Too much secret. North woman me. Fethonite." With this she pointed at Hesteon and Teon. Hesteon had already fallen asleep on a bench. The exertions of the day and the shock of the fall and the broken ankle had taken its toll. She continued. "Alone, we. Travellers. Important." She stopped, and suddenly her face, then voice, changed to almost pleading. "Me, trust, please. Tell more none."

Mayrog sat for many minutes looking from Anga to Teon to Hesteon. He was aware somehow that there was something very important here, that this slip of a Northern girl, this man with the broken ankle and this boy, so badly injured he was lucky to be alive, were very special. He thought again. Perhaps the older man was also an accessory to what was happening here, just as he, Mayrog, was. But in the lad and the girl there was something extraordinary. There was even a part of Mayrog telling him that he was touching something – he struggled to find the words – mystical perhaps, or supernatural. Mayrog turned it around in his mind but could make no sense of it. A girl from an alien race. A boy so badly injured it was a miracle he was alive. Mayrog thought further – no, he recognised the signs, this boy wasn't just injured, he had been beaten. Very badly beaten. His suffering was no accident: someone had done this to him. Perhaps the beating had been several days or even weeks before, but he had, at some time, taken a horrific beating. Logically he just could not see how these two young people could be as extraordinary as he felt them to be. Yet the feeling persisted. At last he responded to Anga. "Anga, I will trust you."

Anga smiled at Mayrog, the same dazzling smile she had given to the children moments before. It was a smile that lit up her face, and confirmed even more deeply in Mayrog that here was something remarkable. "Anga thank you," she said. Her face became serious again.

After several moments of quiet, Anga spoke again, pointing to Hesteon. "You heal man. Care here. We travel tomorrow. Don't hear us. Let us go."

Mayrog paused again looking at Anga. "Let me get it right, what you are asking. You want us to care for the older man, but you and the lad are to travel on tomorrow?" Anga nodded. Mayrog was uncertain. "The lad is very ill, and badly injured. He may not survive any more journeying. Can you expect us to let him go? We are good people and we care. We want to help him."

Again there was silence. Suddenly they heard Teon move in front of the fire and all looked to him. He spoke in a whisper. "Tomorrow. Before dawn the two of us go."

Mayrog paused, then spoke. "If you must go, our menfolk will come with you. The journey will be dangerous and we will guard you and carry you. We will not let you go on alone."

Anga's anger again returned. "Too many. Small party. You warriors. No warriors. Me and Him". Anga pointed to Teon.

Mayrog interrupted Anga's sudden tirade. "You will not make it to anywhere. We will not let you go without us." Mayrog turned to look at Teon. He spoke quietly. "If you go alone he will not survive".

Teon suddenly looked up and returned Mayrog's stare. Teon spoke with a whisper that everyone heard. "You cannot come. We go alone." With that Teon rolled over, wincing with pain. In seconds he was asleep. There was no more to be said.

16

The next morning it was raining hard, the raindrops drumming on the tent. Jayron woke to the sound of riders and horses, and after listening to the rain for a few moments went outside. It was a small group of messengers from the Bayronites. Jayron went to meet them personally. Only one of them dismounted and he spoke to Jayron with an arrogant officious tone to his voice. He had to inform Jayron that Magrell would meet with him at the throne of Fethon at one hour after midday. He would meet to accept his surrender, and to witness his signing of the documents that would make Fethon part of the Bayronite empire.

Jayron's guard was upset by the tone of the man, and the notion that Magrell's messenger was somehow giving orders to Jayron. He reached in anger for his sword to strike at the messenger. Jayron, however, raised his hand to calm and silence him. He spoke to the messenger. "Tell Emperor Magrell that I will be there at the time he has given". With that the messenger pointedly did not bow to Jayron, rather turned and mounted his horse, and with the rest of his patrol rode east towards the Bayronite forces.

Jayron called together the leaders of his army. His mind was racing back to the night before, to the candle, the face, the voice. "Gentlemen" – he spoke to his leaders – "There is one further order I would like issued to every soldier in our army as soon as possible". His voice emphasised the last few words. "It is this – if anything the slightest bit unusual happens through this day, I must be informed of it. There is nothing that must be kept from me. Do you understand? Absolutely nothing." Again his voice emphasised his final words. The soldiers though puzzled, nodded, then went to their troops.

Magrell rose late that morning, and took a leisurely breakfast. He had sent messengers to Jayron to say he would be at the throne an hour after midday, but he planned to arrive at least two hours later than that. To make Jayron wait would increase his humiliation at Magrell's hands, and increase Magrell's sense of power.

The first part of the morning was spent in preparation for the march into Fethon. A section of his army, his logistics group, would remain here on the border as a staging post for supplies into Fethon and for booty to be taken back to Gresk. However, many of the tents were taken down and loaded into carts, as were many of their supplies. The rain made the task a depressing one, particularly after the party they had had the previous day, but there was a confidence about the Bayronites that made the task of packing pass quickly. It was also obvious to Magrell that the rain would make little difference to their travelling – the road from Fethon to Bayron was extremely good, the hard surface made with sandstone. It might be a touch more slippery but the sandstone would still give a good grip: the rain would make little difference to them.

At mid morning the troops began to move towards Durringham. The cavalry went first, then the foot soldiers interspersed with the supply wagons. Then came the personal carriages for the leaders – Magrell, Haren, the other leaders of the army. Finally came a rearguard of the cavalry. Magrell looked proudly along his well-equipped army, numbering up to 20,000 soldiers. It was a force he knew no-one, particularly the Fethonites, could resist.

The journey was uneventful. It felt little more than a stroll in the country. Magrell smiled at his own joke: it was a stroll in the country – someone else's country! The Bayronites passed through a number of villages, all of which were deserted: the residents had all fled to the capital. Small groups were detailed to loot what they could from the villages. Where there was little to loot the villages were put to the torch by the raiding groups – almost out of a perverse revenge for not yielding any profit. At midday the forces stopped at the fork in the road – straight on leading to Durringham, right leading around the north of the city to the throne of Fethon, and ultimately joining the road north from Durringham to the Northern wilderness.

Magrell had already made his plans. He sent his foot soldiers on along the road to Durringham. They would take up positions around the South, south west and south east of the city so that no-one could escape. He took the cavalry and supply wagons along the road to the throne of Fethon where they would meet with Jayron and set up camp. Magrell had already decided where he would set up his own tent for best symbolic impact. He would camp on the very centre of the Throneland.

Jayron spent the morning with his counsellors. Again and again they reviewed the situation. Again and again it seemed hopeless. Jayron too felt the despair of the situation, but perhaps what they saw was not the whole picture. The events of the night before when he had seen the face gave him a glimmer of hope. Together Jayron and the counsellors planned how they could save as many of their people as possible, how least damage could be done to the land. They planned to meet with Magrell and give him a number of requests before surrendering, hoping that Magrell would honour some sort of agreement. They were sceptical even of that, but there was little more they could do.

At midday Jayron and his counsellors, from their vantage point, saw the Bayronite troops at the fork in the road, and watched the footmen continue towards Durringham. They watched the cavalry and supply wagons turn up the road towards the Throneland. Within half an hour, the Bayronite cavalry began to gather on the opposite side of the amphitheatre. They watched the supply carts move onto the land between the throne and Durringham – a flat plain of well-drained land, cutting off the throne of Fethon from the city.

The time for the meeting between Jayron and Magrell came and went as the Bayronite forces flooded in increasing numbers into the area. Jayron registered that the agreed time passed but there was little he could do as he waited on the western edge of the Throne land. His city was rapidly becoming surrounded. The centre of his throne here at the Throneland was quickly being taken over by the Bayronites. Already the Bayronites were setting up camp at the very door of the capital city.

At last Jayron saw the ornate coach that he assumed belonged to Magrell approaching the circle, pulled by four white horses. He watched as the coach stopped and Magrell climbed out. He watched as Magrell walked around to his generals, reviewed some of his cavalry. Within minutes the two would meet. Within minutes Fethon would be lost.

"Sir". Jayron turned to see who spoke to him. Jayron saw one of his captains of guard standing there. Jayron nodded for him to continue, then turned back to watch Magrell's coach, listening only vaguely to the soldier.

"Sir, you asked us to report anything that was out of the ordinary. I don't know if this means anything."

"If what means anything?" Jayron spoke curtly.

"Sir, two strangers have come to the camp, mere children, sir. One badly injured, sir. One an alien girl, sir." The soldier started to lose his nerve and began jabbering to the king. "We were going to send them away, sir, when the injured boy spoke to us."

Jayron was already beginning to regret his order of the morning that anything unusual should be reported to him. He had already heard about horses bolting, groups of birds flying in "odd" formations, a soldier throwing three consecutive sixes in a game of dice, as well as what seemed like a hundred other irrelevancies. "Spoke to you?" Jayron replied, barely showing interest, not even looking to the soldier. "What did he say?"

"Sir", the soldier looked around nervously. "Sir, the boy said: "Tell the king the chosen one is here". That's all, sir."

The soldier suddenly looked frightened as the king turned sharply and animatedly towards him. Jayron stared hard at the captain, then spoke abruptly. "Said what?"

"Sir", the guard had become very frightened, taking Jayron's sharpness as a sign of anger. "The boy said: "Tell the king the chosen one is here". Sir, you said to report anything strange, anything…"

Jayron held up his hand and stopped the soldier, his mind in a whirl. The face. The candle. The voice that had spoken to him. He calmed the sudden beating of his heart, and said to the soldier: "Take me to them."

17

Early in the morning, well before dawn, Anga woke from her sleep. She was grateful the north people had such a sense of time, and that for several days she had been rising from sleep early to go to Golo. As she moved around quietly preparing for the journey – packing food, their few belongings, taking Hesteon's things from the bags, Mayrog appeared. To one side of the main room was a door that led to an anteroom, and off that room were the family bedrooms. Mayrog, that night, had allowed Hesteon to sleep in his bed. He had waited until Anga and Teon were asleep in the main room, a sleep that came to them quickly in their exhaustion, then had opened the door to the main room and slept in the anteroom – he would not miss them in the morning – he would not let them sneak out without him.

As Anga prepared for the journey, she was suddenly aware that Mayrog was in the room with her. He spoke quietly to Anga: "I will help you prepare". Quietly he helped Anga by packing a bag of food for the journey. He also retrieved the donkey from the out-houses, then helped Anga load the donkey. Finally they roused Teon, helped him to eat, then wrapped him in rugs and set him on the donkey.

At last Mayrog had spoken. "I must go with you. You cannot do this alone."

Anga became very agitated. "No soldier. Go alone. Not you. Him. Alone. Anga."

Mayrog was not to be put off. "I must go. You will not manage alone." Mayrog, large and powerful, stood in the doorway preventing Anga from leaving the house.

Anga was becoming more agitated and more upset as they stood there arguing in whispers: this was wasted time. Anga wanted to be travelling. She wanted to leave early as the day would be long; their goal was still far distant. Suddenly she picked up a chair that stood beside the door, whirled it around her head and brought it crashing down on Mayrog's head. Mayrog had not seen it coming quickly enough, cried out, then slowly crumpled to the floor. The chair fell to pieces in Anga's hands.

Anga dropped the back of the chair and was quickly through the door. She caught hold of the donkey's rope and headed as quickly as she could into the darkness of the hour before dawn.

Mayrog's family were woken by Mayrog's scream and the loud crash of the chair. They quickly gathered in the main room of the house. Mayrog's wife Rayda took in the open door, the crumpled heap, the broken chair. She moved across to the crumpled heap on the floor who was her husband. Having kicked the door closed, she lifted Mayrog onto one of the benches and sent her son to get cold cloths. There was a trickle of blood coming from the back of his head and he was dazed, but the injury was not serious. He was coming around from the blow, and clutched his head which clearly hurt.

For several minutes Mayrog sat there until his head began to clear, while Rayda mopped it with cold cloths. Finally Rayda spoke to him. "That evil little bitch..." Mayrog raised his hand to stop her.

"No, no, wait." He said thoughtfully. His mind was churning through the events since the night before as he sat on the bench holding his head. "No, there was something going on there. Something beyond us. Beyond all of us. I hope I know one day what was happening. She asked us to trust her and I said I would. We must let them go – let's just clear up the mess." Rayda said no more and kept her thoughts to herself both out of respect for her husband and a sense that he could be right – she too had sensed something in the boy the night before when she had tended his wounds. As she began to clear the broken chair they heard someone enter the room from the anteroom hobbling across the main room.

Hesteon stood there. "Where are they?" He asked angrily. No one replied as Hesteon looked towards the door and guessed that the other two had left without him. He looked at Mayrog. "Damn their hides" he spat out in annoyance. But it was an annoyance laced with affection.

The rain made the journey miserable. Overnight Teon had recovered some of the energy he had lost the previous day. Teon smiled ironically – recovered enough to feel the cold rain trickling down his neck. He also knew that now there was only him and Anga. And the donkey. Teon reflected – that was how life was – he got a bit better through the night of sleep and then was even worse by the next night. He was once again on the loathed donkey. One day he hoped he would never have to ride a donkey ever again but could not believe the day would ever come. Even if he lived. Teon mentally checked around his body, checking out his injuries. Little was different: his useless arm and fingers, the bruising on his face and chest, the hacking cough he could not throw off. Worse, Teon clearly felt he was getting worse and not better. This morning he knew he was worse than the previous one. Which was worse than the previous one. Which was....A thought occasionally passed through his mind – how many more mornings could he take before he was dead? He knew it could not be many.

As they journeyed on in the darkness they passed through a number of villages and settlements, once or twice disturbing dogs, once hearing a woman shout, but if anyone looked out there was nothing but darkness to see – the moon of the previous night well blocked by the clouds that were sending the unrelenting rain.

They made slow progress as they travelled through the darkness. The darkness and rain dampened both their spirits, and neither spoke as they travelled. Finally they saw the first light rising to their left. Their spirits lifted now that the new day was about to break on them. As the light came they saw a village ahead, a village that seemed to have a strange atmosphere. No smoke from chimneys. No sound of animals. No voices. The village seemed dead. As the path led into the village they could sense that the village really was dead, that all the residents had fled, taking livestock with them. Toys lay in gardens, a handcart was left on the street, but there was no doubt that the people had all left in haste.

As they continued their slow progress they passed through other settlements, and it was the same at each, no people, houses locked, sometimes houses ransacked. The people had clearly fled their homes, although most seemed to have had enough time to lock homes and prepare for whatever had happened.

Anga and Teon continued along the path over the plains, moving south further into Fethon. As daylight came they began to move more quickly, moving with more certainty on the rock-strewn path. They continued in silence, not knowing why this was the right way to go, but certain that they had chosen the right route – there was no other route to choose. By midmorning the path seemed to be heading to a small tree-covered hill that they would have to pass over, the trees part of a greater forest that stretched out to their right. Perhaps half an hour after noticing the wood they were entering the trees. The path was surrounded by pine trees, giving little visibility ahead, soon leaving them feeling very alone as their visibility shortened to perhaps fifty yards either way. They occasionally saw a buck of some type crossing their path, heard the rustle of an animal or bird away to the side, but generally the pine trees remained silent. Teon felt cheered as he saw a red squirrel – the first he had seen since his days back in Mayeringham – such a dim, distant and painful memory: he wondered whether Mayeringham had ever existed.

Anga had spoken to Teon briefly as they entered the wood. "Stop hilltop. Rest."

The path rose slowly but was easy for the donkey and Anga – smooth, covered with pine needles, easier than the rockstrewn path they had journeyed over earlier. Within forty minutes they reached the top of the hill and the path dropped away ahead of them. It was as they rested they smelt something wrong.

For a few moments they thought it was just the pine forest, the smell of pine trees, but there was something more. The smell of smoke drifted through the pine trees. It was a smell that slowly grew stronger. For several long minutes they puzzled at the smell. "We must go and see. We must go quietly", whispered Teon.

The path down the other side of the hill through the trees was as good as the path to the hilltop, so Teon held onto the donkey and began to walk: his walk little more than a limping stagger. The path was gentle – more hard-pressed soil covered with pine needles, a surface that not even the rain could make a difference to. As they walked slowly the smell of smoke became stronger and stronger. It was far stronger than you would find with a bonfire. Within minutes they saw wisps of smoke creeping through the trees. Soon they could hear the sound of flames crackling, see through the trees the occasional flame leaping in the distance.

Slowly they continued. Now they could hear sounds of men's voices cheering, laughing on the breeze. Suddenly they could see the grassland again through the trees, and could see houses ahead burning. They could see soldiers – Teon noticed immediately that these were Bayronite soldiers, with torches setting fire to the houses, one after another. They suddenly heard a number of people screaming, followed by a long shuddering scream of a woman's voice, a scream that stopped as abruptly as it had started.

Teon and Anga stood in the trees watching, unseen by the soldiers in the village. A few moments later the awful screaming began again – they knew from just one person. As they watched a figure ran from behind one of the burning buildings – probably a woman. It only took ten seconds to be sure it was a woman and to see that the woman's clothes were on fire. They watched horrified as she began to run up the path towards them, the flames engulfing her as she ran, the woman screaming out in pain and fear. They could hear the soldiers laughing as she ran.

Her step became more and more of a stumble as she ran up to the path to the pine trees, her voice screaming, carrying through the forest. False hope told her the forest would be sanctuary. The soldiers laughed all the more as they watched. Within seconds she had passed Teon and Anga in their hiding place, running deeper into the forest. Then they heard her voice die out and they saw her fall slowly to her knees, then fall on her front, the flames now dying out.

Anga grabbed their water from the donkey and ran after the woman, unseen by the Bayronites. She poured the water onto any remaining flames and they quickly went out. She crouched and turned the woman gently onto her back. Anga heard a faint gurgling noise in her chest. The woman's eyes stared unseeing into the sky. Anga also saw the deep wound in the woman's stomach, probably made by a spear, the blood seeping out onto the ashen clothes. Within seconds the gurgling was gone, as life left the woman lying at Anga's feet.

Anga slowly stood up and returned to Teon. Teon noticed her face was deathly white as she whispered to Teon. "Woman. No help. Bad." Both remained hiding in the shrubs.

After perhaps twenty minutes they saw the soldiers mount their horses and ride off to the South, the same way as Teon and Anga were travelling; in seconds they were gone.

Anga and Teon emerged from the trees horrified by what they had seen. They followed the path to the village along which the woman had come only minutes earlier. The houses were still burning, though some were now just smouldering. Even the rain could not seem to dampen the strength of the fires. It was as they passed the first house they began to see the bodies. A blood-spattered young man – lying on the ground. A child with vacant face resting obscenely over a horse trough. An old woman with throat cut still half sitting on a bench. There were others. In silence Teon and Anga counted perhaps twenty bodies – men, women and children. There may well have been others they did not see, and from the earlier screams they had both guessed that some had been burned alive in their own homes. It was clearly a village that had decided to stay, rather than leave as the others had done. Perhaps thinking they could disappear into the trees if threatened. Perhaps thinking they could fight back. Thinking that they would not be bothered. It was the worst decision they had ever made. The village – houses and people – all were no more.

Mayrog gingerly turned to Hesteon – his head still hurt. "Come, sit down". He beckoned for Hesteon to come and sit at the table. Hesteon hobbled over with the help of his crutch and took the seat opposite Mayrog. Mayrog smiled ruefully at Hesteon for a moment and spoke again. "She is some woman, that girl", and rubbed his head carefully. Mayrog's smile went just as quickly as he continued. "My friend, they are gone. They would not let me travel with them." Mayrog rubbed his head again. "They told me to look after you. I do not know where, but they are gone. Perhaps travelling to Durringham. I am sorry I let them escape us here."

Hesteon was quiet for some time, so Mayrog continued. "My Friend – I'm sorry I don't even know your name – what is all this about? In those two young people I feel I have been in the presence of greatness. What is going on here?" For a moment he eyed Hesteon quizzically, then spoke again, his voice changed. "No, you tell us in a moment. We must be good hosts – first let us have food, let us have breakfast."

The women of the house busied themselves preparing food, the men preparing for the work of the day. The pause gave Hesteon time to think, time to think how much he could say, how much he had to leave out. He knew now that the two youngsters had to go, and knew that at the moment they no longer needed him, particularly since he had broken his leg the evening before. He had got them this far. The rest was up to them. Whatever the rest might be. He also knew he dare not name his son, or even, at this time, let on that he knew who he was. He could not, at this moment, tell these people anything about Teon.

At last Hesteon and the family sat around the table to eat. Hesteon counted ten of them – Mayrog, his wife Rayda, and the other eight – sons, daughters and their spouses. The children had all eaten as the breakfast had been prepared. Most of them were outside playing; two or three remained to look at this stranger and listen to what he had to say. Rayda introduced Hesteon to the people sat around the table but there were so many of them – he knew he would not remember them. It was Mayrog who talked first, telling Hesteon about the invasion and war, and the events as the people of Fethon understood them to be. He told of a stupid boy call Teon who had started all the trouble. People suggested that at best he was "funny in the head". Mayrog explained that they thought they were far enough from where the battles might be, where the Bayronite's might come, that they had stayed in their settlement, and if the Bayronites did come they could probably escape onto the high plateau. Hesteon knew something of the origins of the story, but the events surrounding the invasion had passed him by – much of that had taken place while he was at the commune, then later on the journey over the high plateau with Teon and Anga. Mayrog finished: "And now my friend – we still do not know your name – what can you tell us of your story".

Hesteon was grateful to Mayrog for talking – it gave him the chance to make sense of some of the things he did not understand, and make clear in his mind what he could and could not say. He had also heard Teon mentioned contemptuously so knew he was right to say nothing further about him. He also appreciated Mayrog's question "What can you tell us of your story," giving him permission to leave out what he could not say.

Hesteon began his story carefully. "My name is Hesteon and I was in Gresk. I had been injured, and was taken to the sanctuary of a healing commune on the edge of Gresk". Hesteon felt he could tell nothing of why he had been at Gresk, or of what had happened before. He desperately wanted to talk about Gowli as part of his mourning for her, but even that would be too risky, too many chances for a slip of the tongue if they asked about her. He went on to tell how he had met the lad who had been badly injured – he did not dare to name Teon – at the commune, that he had been asked to bring him to Fethon. To the family's questions he told them he didn't even know the boy's name. He told how they had travelled the northern path, aware of what might be happening further south. He talked of the High Plateau and how they had met the north people. He talked of Anga joining them, and their journey to the settlement here. He mentioned nothing about Teon being called the chosen one – it would have sounded too bizarre and may have made these people ask more questions, awkward questions. Mayrog and his family did ask many questions. Each one Hesteon answered carefully to give nothing more away. They wanted to know more about the north people. More about Gresk. More about their journey to the plateau. More about the lad. They had all travelled on the plateau in the past and had even stayed in the hut, but few people made the journey into the grim no-man's land, and it was some years since any of Mayrog's family had been.

Hesteon, Mayrog and Rayda talked all morning and through lunch, Hesteon being very careful to tell nothing more than he had already. The rest of the family were in and out, sometimes sitting listening, other times about the chores of daily living. The children quickly became bored with the adult chatter, and had left to play in the barns. Hesteon knew he had to protect Teon's identity – to reveal his true identity would have caused too much confusion, too many problems. Perhaps it was simply that these people would know that Teon had caused the invasion. Several times they referred to Teon in scathing tones; each time Hesteon said nothing, biting his lip hard as his desire to defend his son leapt to his heart.

It was at the end of lunch that Rayda – a direct and penetrating questioner, asking many questions through the morning – dropped the question they had all been avoiding. "What shall we do?" She looked long and hard at Hesteon and spoke again. "I know you have only given us half the story and will tell us nothing more, and perhaps you have spoken some lies as well" – Hesteon grimaced but said nothing to Rayda's penetrating insight. She continued after a brief pause: "It is perhaps not our business to know more, not good to know more. I do know that what is going on here is good. But: what shall we do?"

The question was greeted with silence – no-one could decide what they should do.

It was Rayda herself who answered the question, saying more than she had said since Hesteon had met her. "We all know we have been touched by something special last night." She paused. She pointed at Mayrog's head and smiled "Some have been more touched than others". Again she paused, then continued more seriously: "We all know our lives will never be the same. We know that those two young people are the centre of something phenomenal, or will be. I would like to see it. We must go to Durringham."

No-one spoke for some minutes, then all spoke at once. "How can we go?" "We must get food." "Can we leave the settlement?" "How far is the journey?" "What about the Bayronites?" "Isn't it dangerous?" The clamour continued as all ten people tried to speak at the same time. Finally Mayrog banged the table and they fell silent.

Mayrog spoke. "Rayda is right. We must go. Or at least I must go. Two of our families, you with the children" – he pointed to two couples at the bottom end of the table "must stay here to look after our settlement and home. The rest of us will journey – we can pack food in moments. We will take four of the horses. Our friend Hesteon can ride on one with his damaged leg, we will share the other three. They did not want us to follow, but I think we have no choice."

Twenty minutes later the party set out on the road that Anga and Teon had taken just six hours before.

18

The smoke in the village caused Teon to break into yet another coughing fit. Each one not only seemed to weaken him but hurt the bruising, the broken ribs in his chest. Anga seemed to take little notice, but pulled the Donkey as quickly as she could through the village to escape the horrors they were seeing. Within minutes they were through the other side and on the track to Durringham.

For three, perhaps four hours, Anga and Teon continued along the road that they suspected led to the Fethonite capital city. Anga kept a watch for other bands of soldiers who may have been active in that part of the country, but they encountered none. Occasionally they stopped to eat a little of the food Mayrog had packed, and to drink from a stream. Sometimes Teon and Anga spoke to each other but both were feeling under huge dark clouds. For Teon the rain, added to his cough and injuries had depressed his spirits and health. For Anga it was the sheer horror of having seen the woman die at her feet.

Anga and Teon also gained from Magrell's arrogance. In his belief that the task of taking Fethon would be easy, he had not really planned or felt he needed to block and patrol the roads. He knew of the Northern route but knew that simply led back to Gresk. He knew that no-one would want to head to the barbaric and cruel North People: the only feeling people had for them was fear. He also knew that Jayron was no coward – he knew that Jayron would not run as long as one citizen of his was left in Fethon. There was no point in blocking the roads because Jayron would not run away. Magrell had sent out a few patrols to begin terrorising and looting the land – it was one of these that Teon and Anga had seen at the village – but he felt no need to take any great care in fear of Fethonites escaping, and the full-scale rape of the country could follow Jayron's surrender.

As they travelled further along the road, Anga and Teon became increasingly alert to the sound of activity drifting towards them on the wind from the South. Men shouting. A horse whinnying. They had stopped once, looked at each other, Anga had shrugged her shoulders, then continued leading the donkey towards the sounds which became more persistent as they travelled. The further they travelled the more constant the noise became, the noise of an army, or armies, gathered. At last they reached a turn in the road and saw ahead of them a group of soldiers, standing guard on the road. Soldiers that could have been Fethonite or Bayronite. As Teon and Anga continued along the road towards the guard post, they realised that this was probably a Fethonite post flying the Fethonite flag. Probably Fethonite, but they could not be certain the Bayronites had not taken over the post.

The guards stood firm on the road watching this strange sight come down the gentle slope of the road towards them. So strange it took them many minutes to make out the two figures, one riding on the donkey. As the small group came closer they looked even more bizarre. The figure walking was a young woman, perhaps even a girl. On the donkey was a young, thin, man with badly overgrown hair and whispy beard, who looked horribly ill, in very poor condition. As they approached even closer the soldiers noticed the girl was alien, her skin colour different from the people either of Fethon or Bayron.

"Halt, in the name of the king", the first guard ordered and Anga and Teon came to a halt about five yards from them. Approaching the guards had been nerve-wracking for Anga and Teon: nerve-wracking even though they were hoping approaching guards from Fethon. When the guard spoke it confirmed to Teon and Anga that these soldiers were Fethonite – only Fethon had a king. The guard spoke again: "Throw down your weapons and identify yourselves."

Anga shouted back: "No have weapons".

The guard said to the other: "call those three over there to cover" – he pointed to a small group of soldiers perhaps thirty yards away. They quickly joined the guards, watching the strange characters in front. Anga helped Teon off the donkey and set him on a rock beside the track – the strength of his legs once again deserting him. The sergeant – the leader of this group of guards, drew closer to investigate. He said nothing as he searched their bags. He turned to Anga and Teon. He found they had no weapons – just a small knife in their bag for preparing food. They barely had anything at all, only a little of the food they had collected at Golo remaining.

"Who are you?" He spoke in the same military voice, but a little quieter. He beckoned to the other soldiers to join him. "Well? Who are you?" He barked.

Teon looked up and whispered. "I must see the king".

The soldier stared for a moment, then he laughed. "The king does not talk to boys like you. The king is far too busy to see you. The king has far too much on his mind to worry about the likes of you".

Anga, still standing, turned to the soldier. She shouted, her temper instantly roused by the soldier's refusal. "King. Talk king. King. Want King." She stopped as Teon reached out his good hand and tapped her on the back.

Teon looked at the soldier, then whispered again: "Tell the king the chosen one has come." As he spoke his eyes bored into the soldier. The soldier was taken aback by the fire piercing right into him from those eyes.

The soldier thought for a few moments, then said to his comrades "Guard them. I will see if I can speak to the king. The king has told us to report anything unusual."

The soldiers waited and the two teenagers waited, Teon suddenly remembering that the rain had stopped some time ago. Within minutes the soldier had returned with the king. The soldiers were surprised: the king seemed very agitated. Until now Jayron had shown nothing but strength to his soldiers, but now there was something different. He appeared almost excited as he joined the small group. "There he is, sir", said the soldier, pointing at Teon.

The king gestured for the men to step back, then knelt in front of Teon. He could see the awful condition Teon was in. Jayron's voice was strong as he spoke. "You said you are the chosen one. You are in such.... You cannot be."

For perhaps a minute there was silence as Teon felt overwhelmed to be in the presence of his king. For Teon, the king – Jayron – was an awesome figure whom he had thought he would never meet. Then Teon spoke again in his hoarse whisper. "I must speak to Magrell. I want you to see. I want many to see. I must speak to Magrell." Teon had not even realised until now what he had to do, but he knew he must talk to Magrell. He didn't know why, or even what he would say, just that he must meet Magrell publicly.

Jayron replied quietly. "I don't think that will be possible...."

Anga's voice broke in angrily. "Must. Magrell. Him say. Him do. He know. Him chosen." Her voice stopped as quickly as it started as the king looked at her.

Jayron looked hard at the strange young woman with her eyes flashing anger, then back to Teon. In Teon Jayron could see fire, light, an energy far beyond human energy. From Teon's eyes he could feel the fire flashing through him, through his body. This boy who hardly had the energy to speak, not even the strength to stand had burnt into his very being. In that moment Jayron had changed his entire plan for his dealings with the Bayronites. This boy would be given a chance to speak to Magrell. In front of a large audience. In a way that all could hear.

Jayron called for a covered stores cart and himself lifted Teon inside. Anga climbed in and sat beside Teon. Teon lay resting on some sacks and quickly fell asleep. Anga sat with Teon holding his hand, resting his head in her lap – she knew that for Teon sleep was the only strengthener, the only healer he had at this time. For Anga the afternoon was the first time she had time to think. And cry. She had seen more horror in the last three days than in the rest of her life. She had seen people suffering illness and injury in the past – it was part of life in the North Lands, but always people were given rest and care. She cried for Teon, given no rest and little care in his awful suffering.

Anga felt many different feelings. She felt regret at having to leave her family. She smiled as she remembered hitting Mayrog over the head with the chair, then her feelings turned to regret and she knew she would have to apologise. Mayrog was a good man and did not deserve that. But she hadn't hit him too hard.

She shrugged her shoulders – there was nothing she could do about Mayrog at the moment. Part of her felt sorry to leave Hesteon behind – he had been a strong companion on the journey, but there had been no choice now his leg was broken. Mostly Anga thought about this boy. Teon. Somehow she knew that together they were one. Somehow she knew that together they were destined for something.... She couldn't think what word to use. Together in just two days they had already been through much, seen more than many people would see, experienced more than most people would experience in a lifetime. She knew she was keeping him alive, but only just. She too had recognised that there was a fire in this Teon she had never seen before even amongst her own people. She felt that their destiny was together. Yet Anga could gain no picture of what might happen, what Teon was doing, or what her part was to be in coming events. But she knew that for her at this moment Teon was the most important thing in the world. She cared for him with a passion far beyond duty.

As soon as Jayron had settled the two youngsters in the cart he gave orders that the cart be taken to his palace in Durringham, along with a number of others so as not to arouse any suspicion in the Bayronites at the sight of a single cart moving. Then he called a small handful of his closest, most loyal, advisors together. Things had to be organised quickly: there was little time – barely minutes – until Magrell would appear at the Throneland. He told them that they had to obey his orders. He demanded it of them, however strange the orders may seem. There was no time to explain, but the future of their land depended on their obedience. On their trust. He gave a series of rapid orders to these men. One or two tried to argue – what Jayron was proposing seemed so outrageously bizarre, but Jayron had no time for disobedience. He repeated his orders, and quickly sent the men on their way. Each one knew that what Jayron had ordered sounded absurd, but this was Jayron and he was urgent and confident. Each one would obey. Each knew that Jayron was someone they wanted to trust.

Jayron called his other councillors and ordered them to backup what he had to say when he met with Magrell in their presence – there had been a change in plan. Again he insisted – however strange, they must back what he said. Again he demanded their trust. As loyal as his councillors were, he was uncertain they would go with what was about to happen.

Magrell entered the Throneland at mid-afternoon, two hours later than he had agreed with Jayron, accompanied by his leading ministers and wife Haren. As Magrell walked towards the centre, Jayron too entered the amphitheatre from his camp accompanied by a number of his elders. He had rushed back to the edge of the circle after his encounter with the two young people and the subsequent changes he had made to his plans. The phrase "young people" suddenly jarred on Jayron – he had not even asked their names – but that didn't seem to matter. No longer did he need to find a dignified way to surrender. He could still surrender, but now perhaps there was another way.

Jayron walked into the circle of the Throneland, and the two leaders slowly approached each other. As they approached each other both signalled to their companions, gesturing for them to drop back from the initial meeting. At last they were ten yards apart and facing each other. After a formal and dignified moment Jayron bowed, then spoke. "Welcome, Emperor of the Bayronites to our land of Fethon. We hope you will gain much from your visit to this land." Jayron managed to keep all sound of irony out of his voice.

Magrell stood looking and waited for Jayron to finish. "Cut the rubbish, clown. You are finished". Magrell's voice was laden with contempt. He had hated the Fethonite royal court since that first visit there when he had been bored to tears, along with his "friend" – he smiled as his mind said it: his "friend", Hamlan.

Jayron knew how to keep his dignity. "Emperor, let us call our councillors and plan the programme for today."

Magrell sneered, turned his back and gestured for his councillors to join him. As they began to move across to the two kings so Jayron's councillors – those who were left there – also moved to the centre of the Throneland. Jayron moved to be with them. As he reached them he spoke again with urgency. "Gentlemen, remember we have changed our plans. Allow me to speak – just back me." The councillors again looked at each other knowing that some of their number, Jayron's closest allies, were now no longer there. Something strange was happening. As they recovered their thoughts, Jayron was already returning to the centre of the circle.

As the councillors from the two sides settled, Jayron spoke to Magrell again. "Emperor. It is our tradition that when a brother leader from a neighbouring country visits we invite him to our palace in Durringham. We allow him and his colleagues to feast with us." Jayron's councillors looked briefly to each other as they heard the script changing, but Jayron was continuing.

"At the feast we eat well, and one or two of our people speak, tell stories, and are allowed to speak in praise of the guests. I am aware, my friend, that you may have other things on the agenda later," Magrell sneered again although Jayron again kept all irony out of his voice, "but this evening the gates of our city will be open and we invite you, your councillors and your leading soldiers to come and feast with us."

For several moments there was silence. The Fethonite councillors wondered what this was about, and looked askance at the idea of opening the city gates. The Bayronite councillors also looked curious – many had not been to Durringham before; all of them enjoyed a feast, and this invasion was turning out to be the greatest carnival they had known. Magrell too was thinking. Until now he had simply been leader of the army, and armies had no times for niceties. There was an old Bayronite army saying: "Butcher, and be back for breakfast". Now, however, Magrell was no longer just leader of the army, he was also Emperor, and wanted to be seen behaving with the dignity Emperors should have. Yes, he would eat at Jayron's table. He would hear the speeches saying how wonderful he was. Then he would slaughter the lot. He was certain of one thing: once Jayron had opened the city gates he would never have the opportunity to close them again.

Only Haren, with her wisdom and years of experience as Emperor's wife, was puzzled: this was not normal protocol, but she kept her thoughts to herself.

That afternoon the Fethonite palace worked hard to prepare the feast. Until now the staff of the palace had been paralysed with the fear that had overtaken the whole of Fethon, but to be given a task – to be ordered to fulfil what would be a huge challenge suddenly was giving them new life. Normally they had days to prepare such a feast, but now only three hours, and in the rush their fear was forgotten. Their stores were raided, as were many of the city shops. Finding food and having it ready would be a monumental challenge, but one the staff were more than happy to undertake – anything was better than the awful waiting that Magrell had made them endure and there was a sense that the orders to prepare the feast were given with some purpose and direction. The staff put to the back of their minds the Bayronite army sitting at their doorstep, and took up the challenge with great relish. They had no doubt that they would have a great banquet ready for their king. Late in the afternoon a train of stores wagons entered the city through the northern gate carrying meat, flour, drink, bread. Two young people were hidden in one of the wagons. One – the boy – fast asleep. The other – the girl – holding his head against the bumping. If anything Teon's coughing had worsened with the rain of the morning. The hot sunshine since had not improved things, and every few moments the hack in his chest seemed to wake him, whereupon his body writhed with the pain that was filling him.

The wagons were pulled into the city, then into the grounds of the palace. Only a few noticed that one of the wagons was taken to the side of the palace, where no eyes could see it being unloaded. No-one wondered what was in the wagon – they were too busy with their own preparations.

For the rest of the afternoon Jayron made ready. Some of his councillors thought he had gone mad, and one or two expressed their opinion to each other. Jayron was aware of the strange glances but he ignored them. He had returned to Durringham and spent the afternoon and early evening in the banqueting hall arranging the chairs and tables, then rearranging them again. Jayron had no idea what would happen. He just knew that everyone had to hear. In the end he settled for a semicircular shape, with an open space against one of the long walls. It was the only wall without windows; it was simply covered in cream paint, with pictures of the wildlife of the country hanging at intervals along the walls. As soon as that was agreed, servants quickly set the tables with cutlery, glasses and napkins. All would be ready for the feast.

Magrell had spent the afternoon with, first, his generals, then his councillors. With his generals he had talked about how the troops should be deployed, particularly through the feast, how they would enter the city, how they would be ready to seize the city square and gates at the end of the feast. He also talked with them about how to ensure the doors of the city were never closed again. With his councillors he had talked about which of the Fethonites they should kill to take away any threat – they did not want a rogue "leader" to emerge able to lead a resistance or popular uprising – and whether they needed to massacre, and how many. He also talked about who would remain to establish the rule when Magrell returned to Gresk, what size force of troops they would need, what they would demand of the local residents. Surprisingly it was this latter discussion that roused Magrell to excitement, although he hid it well. The talk of massacres, killing, public executions had roused the madness which had struck him on this campaign. He left the meetings and stamped around his tent for many minutes trying to shake off the rage and bloodlust that was burning within him, before returning to his troops to direct their preparations.

Haren also was walking around her tent but for her it was in confusion. So many different things happening which left her puzzled, unable to make sense of the afternoon, of what was happening around her. Occasionally she stopped to sip some fruit juice, sometimes she would sit, but she was disturbed. Or was it elated? Or was she puzzled? She even sensed that there was a trap here, but could not see what it might be, as much as she allowed the events to whirl around her mind.

Until now the campaign had been boring. It had been predictable. At times it had been brutal – even Ganerr's death had hurt her. It had been what Haren had expected. They had simply marched into Fethon, they had cowed the people, they had taken what they wanted, and they were heading towards the final capture, the massacre that was the conclusion of all these campaigns. Haren hated this way of acting, hated to see the death, the destruction, but she never showed her loathing. It was the way that all nations behaved to other nations. Except Fethon, under Jayron.

Haren had also experienced Magrell's growing violence, and desire for violence. Twice Magrell had punched her – luckily he had not hit her face and she could hide the bruising. If his desire continued to grow then she knew her life would be at risk in the not too distant future. Haren was also frightened by Magrell's growing arrogance. He certainly knew how to control the army, and his arrogance meant that the soldiers would follow him anywhere. At the moment. Or so Magrell thought.

Haren saw it differently – the soldiers as a group remained loyal, but she knew their minds worked even when their whole lives obeyed, and she could see that the minds of the soldiers were coming to hate this campaign – it felt like the arrogance of the adult Bayronites taking sweets from the innocent childlike Fethonites. There was something in the make-up of a true and professional soldier that hates to attack the childlike, the innocent. If Magrell's arrogance continued to grow, even the soldiers would call a halt – sooner or later. Even clearer to Haren – Magrell's arrogance was affecting his judgement – why could he not see that there was something strange happening.

Haren sent for her servant to fetch her more fruit juice. When the drink came she finally sat down. She couldn't get it out of her mind – something strange was happening. Jayron. Why invite them for a feast? It was bizarre. Jayron knew Magrell would kill him, destroy the city. Why open the gates? And about Jayron there had been a confidence, an excitement that wasn't right. Why was Jayron not in depression, gloom about the coming destruction and loss of his country? Was there a trap? Haren knew something was not as it should be, but she could not see where this was heading.

Haren suddenly leapt to her feet, rushed out of the tent and went to find Magrell. She didn't know why, but she was sure that the first problem of changed plans was the disruption to communication. Whatever unfolded in the coming hours, people had to know about it as quickly as possible. If there were new actions, instructions had to get around the Bayronites quickly. If there were more changes of plan, then orders had to get around as quickly as possible.

Haren explained to Magrell that they had to get their communications systems as effective as possible, particularly between the banqueting hall and the soldiers outside. It made sense to Magrell – runners were organised from each troop of soldiers to be in an anteroom to the banqueting hall, ready to receive any messages, any orders.

Haren returned to her tent. The last few weeks had left her in a deep depression. She had lost her son. She had lost her husband whom she had loved deeply. She was married to this brute of a man who pretended to be Emperor now, yet had no real feeling for the dignity of his role. Haren had hidden all of this behind her "serene" exterior. But at this moment, for the first time for weeks, she felt a glimmer of hope. She had no idea why.

19

As the Fethonite troops began to move from the Throneland towards the city in the early evening, another group of people rode down the path from the North. They were ignored by both Fethonite and Bayronite soldiers as the preparations for the "new" plan went ahead at a pace. This time there had been seven of them – four men, three women; one of the men with an injured foot riding on his own, the other six sharing three horses. They had walked much of the route as quickly as they could, but they had wanted to be in the city early so for the final miles they had all ridden. The journey had been uneventful for them, although they too had ridden through the massacred village – the village that they had known as Loban, but was no more. For them the rain had stopped just as they set out, and the "sun following the rain" had provided excellent conditions for riding and travelling in. They had barely stopped on their journey to Durringham. By early evening the sun was surprisingly hot, the rain now only a memory.

Perhaps because of the confusion of the soldiers returning to the city, or perhaps because they looked like a small group of refugees from the country, they were not challenged as they headed through the troops towards the city gate. Hesteon, Mayrog, Rayda and their family members simply joined the columns of people heading to the city and entered in through the northern gates.

As they arrived in the city they spoke to people and several mentioned the strange banquet, how everything was being done differently, how the city gates were to be left open. They asked several of the other people about strangers, or odd occurrences, but apart from the bizarre preparation of the feast no-one had seen or heard of anything else. All were so busy talking about the feast they wouldn't notice anything else. All the people Mayrog asked were more concerned about the apparent changes in plan and how Jayron was behaving in such an odd way, some daring to call him foolish. No-one knew why the changes had been made.

After Mayrog and his family entered the city they peeled away from the main column of soldiers and supply wagons that were heading towards the barracks. They headed towards the city square in front of the palace. The square was already full of refugees. They found a place to one side of the main palace gates which was free, tied their horses to a hitching post and sat to wait. It was Mayrog who asked the question. "What are we waiting for?"

None of them knew. All of them suddenly had no idea why they were there. It was Rayda who spoke. "We are here to wait and see." With that they remained quiet.

That evening Magrell, his councillors and leading soldiers, all gathered at their camp, then paraded into Durringham with their trumpeters playing a fanfair at the city gates. They walked to the palace, and, accompanied by another fanfair entered the castle courtyard where they were greeted by Jayron, dressed in his ceremonial royal regalia. He led the way into the banqueting hall. Jayron's robe of hessian with red bands around the edges gave him, in its simplicity, a true sense of dignity. Of the Fethonites there was a similar number, but they were already seated in the banqueting hall, and rose to their feet as the Bayronites entered, applauding dutifully at a sign from Jayron. There was no warmth in the applause. Jayron showed Magrell to a seat and sat beside him – they sat half way along the chairs, looking towards the empty space in the semi-circle. Palace staff showed the other Bayronites to their seats – Magrell's leading advisors sat to the left and slightly behind Magrell, while the Fethonite nobles sat to the other side of the two leaders. Haren was on the table next to Magrell, but could only see his back from where she sat. In all around two hundred people sat down to eat.

After Jayron welcomed his guests, the staff of the palace served the meal with remarkable efficiency. Neither Jayron nor Magrell said anything to each other. Magrell laughed with the leaders of his army and other favourites. Jayron talked politely with his own comrades.

For Magrell, the food had been magnificent, with game, fresh fruit, fish and sweetmeats, but the drink poor. Durringham had a reputation for being a "dry" palace and this meal was proving it. One glass of wine had been far less than he would have expected, or given, had he been the host. Jayron too was pleased with the food, but the shortage of drink had also been his idea – he knew that the drunker Magrell was to become, the less likely he was to hear what the boy was to say.

What the boy was to say? Jayron had no idea what the boy was going to say. If he remained alive. Part of Jayron thought this was pure madness, part of Jayron hoped against hope that the candle, the face, the boy, the strange girl, the burning eyes – they all meant something. He had no idea what they would say, or what would happen. He couldn't even imagine how they could make a difference. The further through the meal they were, the more Jayron thought he was about to become a laughing stock. He fought against his loss of nerve. But Jayron had no other plan, no plan B, and he had to go through with it, whatever "it" was.

When all finished the meal and the dishes quickly cleared, Jayron's Master of Ceremonies banged on a table with a gavel. In less than half a minute the room was quiet, looking at Jayron who was standing on his feet.

Jayron spoke to the room. "Friends, we welcome our guests from Bayron, and we wish them long and healthy lives. We particularly welcome our honoured guest Emperor Magrell, and hope he will receive all that is his." Jayron raised his glass as in a toast, echoed half-heartedly by the other Fethonites gathered in the room. Only Haren, of the Bayronites, heard the ambiguity of Jayron's words. Jayron continued. "As you know it is our tradition for representatives of the people to welcome visitors, and particularly our honoured guest," Jayron nodded towards Magrell before continuing. "Following a short presentation in honour of our guests we will be serving the wine, spirits and cocktails. We have scoured our country to find the right people. The two we have found are young people. I invite them to come and speak to the assembled crowd. Ladies and gentlemen, this may seem a strange event to you partly because these young people are handicapped, but also because they have asked permission to make their speech differently. They ask you to see this as a drama presented by two very young people to honour our guests, Emperor Magrell, Empress Haren, and the Bayronite leaders."

The Fethonites looked as bemused as the Bayronites at all of this. They were being presented with traditions they had never heard of. Traditions that had never existed in their country. Others held their heads in their hands at the horror of what seemed to be happening. Only Haren felt excited – she had no idea what was happening, but felt something which set her pulse racing.

For several moments the room was quiet, then a large oak door at one end was opened. In walked an alien girl, with dark coloured skin, dressed in a hessian robe. She was struggling to carry another figure in her arms. She walked slowly to the middle of the long wall that was free, then stepped forward to the centre of the semi-circle – opposite both Magrell and Jayron. She lowered the person she was carrying gently to the floor and helped him to stand slowly and shakily on his feet. Again there was a sense of confusion – this boy in his struggles looked so realistic, yet surely he was acting? Only Jayron knew this was reality. Only Haren was sure that this boy was not an actor. The boy was clearly very weak as the alien girl held him upright facing the top table. Not one eye in the room left the mesmeric "performance" of the two young people. Not one voice spoke. The girl brushed his hair out his face and he looked up, straight into the eyes of Magrell.

In the town square Mayrog and his group were watching the events in the square. Mayrog had quickly realised that fear and paralysis had taken over both body and mind of the Fethonites in the city. Magrell's unsubtle psychological warfare – his arrogant march into Fethon – had drained all spirit from the people. Mayrog's group had no idea what was happening at the banquet but here in the square they were feeling increasingly uneasy. They watched as the frightened refugees sat on the ground, on walls, on benches, some in tears, some simply staring into space. They also watched more and more men in long cloaks coming into the square. Some were passing through, some remaining, making little real effort to hide their military uniforms. It was obvious that the Bayronites were flooding the city with their soldiers, ready to take control at the right signal. The city was vulnerable to them. The Fethonites had no defence.

Hesteon and Mayrog talked quietly, talked of the folly of what the Fethonites appeared to be doing. Instead of defending the walls they had simply opened the gates and let the Bayronites in. Allowed their enemy to walk easily into their stronghold unopposed.

Mayrog kept saying – "we must do something". Over and over he muttered to himself: "We must do something". Mayrog could sense an almost mass hysteria at the prospect of the country being overrun by the Bayronites, a hysteria that was in danger of overwhelming those he had travelled to the city with. He felt the mass paralysis that seemed to stop anyone thinking, plotting, finding a way to combat the enemy. Already the Fethonites were defeated without the Bayronites taking up a single weapon.

It was Hesteon who finally responded excitedly. "Fire. I have an idea – fire."

"What do you mean?" Mayrog looked hard at him.

"Fire. Our weapon. I've got an idea. We must leave. We must go east". Hesteon hobbled excitedly to his feet and started to grab the horses and pull them. "Come on, I know, it is better than sitting here. Fire. Our weapon." Unfortunately for Hesteon, as he reached for the horse and grabbed its reins, the horse moved to one side, and Hesteon fell, sprawling full length on the floor crying in pain from his broken ankle.

Mayrog helped Hesteon to his feet. He shook his head slowly: "My friend, there is little you can do at this time. We must wait".

Hesteon became animated and excited again. "No, we must do it. It is all we can do. Someone has got to do something. Fire. It's what we can use." Again, he tried to get to his feet. Again he sprawled full length on the floor.

"Wait". Rayda put her hand on Hesteon's arm to stop him trying to rise again. "Wait. Tell us what you want us to do. We will do it, but you must promise to remain here."

For several minutes, Hesteon told Mayrog and his family what they should do. He repeated it so that they would know, so that they would not fail. He knew it probably wouldn't win the day, but at worst it would sow confusion, at best it might cause some serious damage to the Bayronites. Doing something was better than sitting here and letting the fear overtake them as it seemed to overtake everyone else they met.

After Hesteon had finished describing his idea twice, Mayrog sat quietly, thinking. At last he made the decision. "We will do it" he said slowly. "We will do it, but we must leave the city without rousing suspicions – we must go slowly, we must go one couple at a time".

It was Mayrog and Rayda who had risen to their feet first, apparently without haste, and headed through the narrow streets to the eastern gate. A few minutes later one of his sons and his wife also left, this time by a different road, circling around through back streets also to the east gate. The other couple – Mayrog's daughter and her husband followed shortly afterwards. Hesteon remained in the square by the palace gate alone, certain that no-one had taken any notice of the six people who had just left.

All three couples, after leaving the square, quickly passed through the narrow streets, and gathered together in the shadow of a tavern – the Brown Boar – the opposite side of the street from the Eastern Gate, just as Hesteon had described. They stood watching the Bayronite guards posted on the gate, looking for a way of slipping out of the gate unnoticed. As they waited, they watched one or two canvas covered supply carts come into the city, two or three leave. They also saw two or three carts prevented from leaving, perhaps because they were driven by Fethonites. Then they noticed three canvas covered carts together coming along the main route from the city square. They watched as they saw the group of carts stopped by the Bayronite soldiers, and the soldiers talking to the cart drivers. Clearly the Bayronites wanted no Fethonites, leaving the city that night.

The carts were stopped in the gateway, the rear of the third cart sticking out of the gateway arch into the city, blocking the view of the back of the carts from the Bayronite soldiers.

Mayrog whispered. "Come on. This is our chance. We must take the risk". They rushed the ten yards across to the back of the cart, and in seconds all six had scrambled inside.

A few moments later – presumably the Bayronites had seen the right documents and let the carts go – the small group was out of the city.

The carts continued bumpily along the track towards the supply camp of the Bayronites on the eastern road, a mile beyond the city gate. Mayrog remembered Hesteon's description of this road, remembering that at one point it climbed steeply through a small copse, turning a hairpin towards the top of the climb. He quickly whispered instructions to his family. When the carts slowed and began to turn the corner his family leapt out one at a time and ran into the trees.

Rayda insisted on being last, and had ushered her family out, then dropped to the ground herself. As she began to run for the trees she kicked a stone by accident. Disturbed by the noise, the guard on the third cart turned and saw Rayda running to the cover of the trees. He shouted "Hey! Stop! What are you doing?" Rayda didn't stop, she continued running, but suddenly felt a thud into her shoulder, a thud that knocked her to the ground, rolled her over and over into a gully deep in the trees. As she came to a stop in the wet mud, the pain began to take over her body.

The others watched from the trees as the guard called out, and saw him throw the spear that caught Rayda in her shoulder. They heard the sickening thud, heard Rayda scream out in pain. The spear was dislodged as Rayda rolled over and disappeared into the gully. They watched as the guard leapt from the cart and picked his spear up again, wiping the blood from the metal tip. He looked around for a few moments, then looked back to the cart. The cart had kept going – it was folly to stop on a hill as steep as this. The guard shrugged his shoulders – it was only a woman – then ran after the cart and leapt on the front with the driver. Within minutes they had disappeared.

Mayrog and his family gathered around Rayda to see that her shoulder was shattered by the spear. They dressed it with rags from their clothes, but Rayda still lost a lot of blood and strength. In a whisper she spoke to them: "You must go, finish the task. All of you. I will be safe here." Her family hesitated, but Rayda was even more insistent. "Go, come back and find me when you are done. GO". She spat the last word daring any to defy her. No-one would defy Rayda when she spoke in that voice.

Quietly they left Rayda in the gully and headed back down the track from where they had come. Mayrog noticed that they were now the other side of the Bayronite forces. The carts they had ridden hadn't stopped in the Bayronite camp but had continued: Mayrog guessed the carts must be returning directly to Bayron, to the border, for them not to have stopped. This was better than they hoped – had the carts stopped in the camp they would have had to wait until nightfall and make a run for it. Here they were already clear of the camp. The tents of the Bayronite forces lay between them and Durringham, and away around the north side of Durringham towards the Throneland – the camp stretched as far as they could see. Small groups of soldiers were assembled by each gate of the city. There were reserve troops mustered to the south of the village. All that was left in the camp itself were orderlies, drivers, servants, along with oxen, cart horses and the supply wagons. As the small group overlooked the camp and the land before them, Mayrog and his remaining family found what they had been looking for.

In the banqueting hall the entire room was transfixed by the two young people. Even in their apparent youth and frailty they had a tremendous presence, tremendous charisma. Most thought that they were, as Jayron had said, acting – it was his way of getting them a hearing. One or two noticed the thinness of the boy, noticed the arm that did not move, the bruises on the side of his head. The lank hair. The long whispy beard. Others looked at Anga's dark skin and thought the girl's colour may have been natural, that her hair looked as it had always been, but no-one dared say.

Teon sat on a chair that had been placed there for him, looked slowly around the room, then dropped his head again. He had seen Magrell, and suddenly he knew what he should do. Teon looked up again. He said in his voice, a cross between a whisper, a croak and a cough "I want to tell a story". Since his arrival in Jayron's camp Teon, in those minutes when he was awake, he had worked out something of what he should say. Somehow what he had to say had grown in his mind. Or been given to him....

Teon paused again as the girl, as Anga, sat at his feet. She held the hand of his broken arm. Teon again pulled himself together. "I want to tell a story."

He paused. Magrell looked quizzically towards the boy – there was something vaguely familiar here. The room was utterly

138

silent waiting for Teon, transfixed by the figures in the centre of the semicircle who captured the complete attention of everyone there. Then Teon began, in the same broken voice he had used before.

"Once there was a son of a great landowner who had everything he wanted, far more than he could use". Teon spoke very slowly, pausing now and then as another cough came to him, but his voice had the room mesmerised. There was a presence about Teon that forced people to listen. Teon continued.

"But his son wanted everything his father had and wanted what his neighbour had as well. He took one of his neighbour's children captive. He killed his own father and tied his neighbour's child to the corpse. The child was blamed, the child was beaten, the child was tortured, the child was killed and put in a grave." Teon's voice was growing in strength as he spoke, although the room still had to work to listen. Teon was in full flow, putting all of his remaining energy into his story. "The Son went to his neighbour to beat him and killed him because of what his child had done. But the child had not done it." Teon's suddenly took on a sorrowful tone. "The neighbour was weaker. The neighbour was killed. His family was butchered. His lands were taken. The Son had everything that belonged to his Father. Everything that belonged to his neighbour." Again Teon paused, then spoke into the complete silence. "Surely there would be justice. Surely there would be a saviour. Surely someone would come and the Son be found in his guilt, captured, punished?"

Magrell had heard these sorts of stories before – he was too confident to understand what Teon was talking about. It was a typical "hero" story: make up some horrific story, then allow the great person to come and save the day and bring justice. He knew the story would end with him as the saviour, because the story was by the Fethonites to pay tribute to the neighbouring Emperor.

Jayron listened too, totally confused, knowing this was out of his hands, aware that something was happening here that he could not understand. He watched as Teon tried to stand to his feet, but stumbled and fell to the floor. Then Anga held him, and he struggled to standing again, this time the girl holding him slumped in her arms. Teon held steady for a moment, then coughed several times. Jayron was about to go to his help, frightened he would not be able to finish. He stepped back in the face of Anga's stare.

As the coughing eased, Teon mustered up all his energy. He twisted in the girl's grip and raised his good arm and pointed directly at Magrell, his eyes burning straight towards him.

At last he spoke, struggling to get the words out, looking straight at Magrell "There was no saviour.

Magrell.

I am Teon.

You are that son."

After walking back along the track for perhaps ten minutes, Mayrog and his family looked at the area on either side of the track – exactly as Hesteon had described it. It was an area the Fethonites called "The Heather Spur". There was common land to the North, and a spur of that heather covered common land came south and crossed the eastern road. A couple of miles to the North the spur of heather covered moor was cut off from the main moorland by a small river that had its roots far away in the high plateau. It tumbled down the rock face, then cut a gorge through the moorland before heading south to the sea.

It was Hesteon who had realised both that the wind had been blowing all day from the East, and that heather was incredibly flammable. He knew that it had rained all morning, but he also knew that the afternoon sun would have dried the heather, heather that before today hadn't had rain for several weeks. He also remembered that this area often caught fire in high summer, with the fires surrounding Durringham but never harming the city – the walls kept the fire at bay. Set fire to the heather, and the flames would be spectacular. They would engulf the scattered trees and corpses, would engulf the dry grass surrounding Durringham, would engulf the rhododendron's surrounding the city walls. Surely, if they could make the fire take, it would have some impact on the events of which they were a part. They had no idea of what impact, but anything was better than doing nothing.

Mayrog and the other men had taken their tinder boxes from their pockets, made small fires about ten yards apart, and tried to set them alight. They tried, but the grass they had to used to make the first flicker of flame had remained damp under the heather. They tried. They rebuilt their fires. Do what they could, they could not get the fires lit. Once lit they knew that the power of fire would be unleashed. They were frustrated – the fires would not take. Mayrog so frustrated he kick out at heather bush, only to have his leg jarred by the soil mound on which it grew.

After half an hour they sat to discuss in a small circle what they should do. It was as they sat that they heard the crackle. Within seconds one of the fires leapt into life. They turned to see the flames leaping in the air – one of them must have got something smouldering which had taken a few minutes to leap into life, but now the life was there, the flames leapt from patch to patch, they could feel the heat. They were aware of the flames leaping wind driven down the road towards Durringham, towards the Bayronites camp. They were also aware that the force of the fire was pushing it their way, and together they began to run back along the track to where they had left Rayda. As they reached the woodlands they knew there was now absolutely nothing more they could do, except let the fire follow its own life. They knew that it would not really harm Durringham – many laughed that the only thing the walls of Durringham would keep out were the summer heather fires – but they watched as it headed for the Bayronite camp.

Inside the banqueting hall Teon had collapsed on the floor again, seeming to have given everything he had. The room remained silent for many moments, then uproar. Fethonites confused, unable to comprehend what was happening. Bayronites angry that their leader had been insulted. Fethonites resigned to their awful fate knowing the Bayronite Emperor had been attacked by the words. The name "Teon" added confusion to many minds. Men were shouting to each other. Some were waving swords. One or two had even made some sense of Teon's story. Only three people remained silent, sat on their chairs. Jayron sat on his chair trying to grasp what was happening in the room, what this young man was about. Magrell sat on his chair deathly white – he had killed this boy, yet here he was back to haunt him. He had no doubt that it was Teon standing there pointing, although now he was crumpled in a heap on the floor. Behind Magrell, Haren also sat quietly. Somehow she felt flooded with light. Her confusion was swept away. In a second she had worked out what Teon had said. She doubted not one word of his story. She even knew that Teon was the child of the story. In seconds she put the whole story together, she knew the monstrosity of what Magrell had done. She looked at his back with utter contempt.

Jayron felt he had to bring order back to the room, so signalled to his pipers to play a fanfare. They had to play three before the hubbub subsided and those in the hall had sat back on their chairs. When all was quiet Magrell had risen to his feet.

"This is monstrous" he roared. "I am accused of I know not what. This boy has cast a slur on me". He turned to Jayron. "What monstrous trick is this? You will pay for your insult. You will pay with your life". Magrell spat in Jayron's face as Jayron stood in front of him.

The room watched the two men staring hard at each other, but then heads began to turn at the sounds of movement from the floor where the boy lay slumped in a heap held by the girl. Teon slowly, with the girl's help, scrambled back onto the chair. The room was transfixed as in some awful peep show, watching a broken man struggling for life, watching Teon struggle to his feet.

For Teon there was something else forcing him to move. Now he had seen Magrell he was remembering. He was remembering the journey to Gresk, the cell, the beatings, being kicked into unconsciousness. He was remembering his friend, Gowli whom he had loved so much. He was remembering his father whose leg was broken, whose spirit had been broken much more harshly. He was remembering the village with the older men killed, the women and children butchered. He remembered the woman set on fire, whom they could not help. And as he remembered anger welled up within him. Anger and hatred welled up against this man, this monster who had destroyed everything that had mattered to Teon. Teon knew that if he had the strength he would have gone over to this man, to Magrell and killed him on the spot for what he had taken from Teon – but Teon didn't have the strength.

Teon forced his legs under him, and with Anga's help sat again on the chair. Anga too felt Teon's anger rising within him. She pinched him hard on his good arm and whispered to him so that only Teon could hear "anger kill you. Not kill him. You stronger."

Not even Magrell could interrupt the real drama happening in front of him. Teon, held up by Anga, opened his mouth to speak again. It wasn't to be – the cough took over his body again, seeming to hack right through him. It forced him to sit down to recover. Magrell had wanted to interrupt but knew he couldn't – all eyes were watching this boy.

For Magrell this boy had just pointed to the first chink in his armour. He knew that this boy had opened the door of his fallibility. He knew that the truth had been given wings, if only the wings of a butterfly. He knew that if he stopped this horror, the curiosity of his people would be roused – they would surely ask what this youth was saying. He knew there would be shame in destroying a child, that if he attacked this child he would be seen not as a powerful leader by his people, but a bully who attacked the injured and weak. Step in now and all the standing, all the respect he had built up in his role in the army, in recent weeks as Emperor would be loosened. Had he stopped this he would be finished; he could only hope that his people, and the Fethonite people, would see this in the end as a publicity stunt, some embarrassing episode that would rebound back onto Jayron, destroying his reputation and standing, not just with his own people, but with his admirers throughout the region.

Teon again stood to his feet, his anger pushing him slowly off the chair. Part of Teon wanted to go to the monster, to Magrell and kill him, beat him lifeless for what he had done to him, to everything that was special to him. He couldn't: partly because he had no real movement in his legs – he could only stand with the help of Anga, but more, he knew there was another way – Anga had told him. As Teon stood there, tears rolled from his eyes, rolled down his face. Tears for Gowli. For His Father. For his country. For all that he had lost. As the tears streamed down Jayron believed that this was the face he had seen in the candle the night before. Maybe it wasn't but the look was so much the same.

Teon again raised his good arm and pointed. At last he felt he had enough energy to speak. His voice was a hoarse whisper. Everyone in the room heard the words. "Magrell. I forgive you."

As Teon spoke, the room crackled with silence. Magrell stood shocked – he had never known anything like this. He knew violence. He knew how to hurt people. He had discovered that he was enjoying hurting people too much. He knew strength, but this was so different, utterly different. He knew the power of strength. Now whirling inside of him he was experiencing the power of weakness.

Suddenly Magrell and the others in the room heard great sounds around them. At first many were puzzled, then quickly realised the sounds were outside the palace. Much of the noise was men shouting in fear, in panic, but there was more. For some it could have been a crowd applauding. For others it may have been water falling. Many of the Fethonites of Durringham knew the sound – the sound of fire was a regular summer event for them. Soon everyone was aware of the fire as the smell of smoke began to seep into the banqueting room.

Magrell turned again to the boy – he knew he faced something more powerful still. He looked at the boy, still pointing at him. As he turned back he heard the crack of sound before anyone else, aware of the bolt of fire that had shot across the room from the boy's finger, the fire that had engulfed him, surrounded him. He felt himself fall to his knees in face of what was happening here. He felt himself touched by a power far greater than his strength and the boy's weakness. Not a fire that burned, or a fire that destroyed, or even a fire that gave him renewed strength. For Magrell it was a fire that showed him a picture, a choice. A fire that said – there is your way, or there is a better way. Then the fire had stopped. Teon too had been stunned by the fire that had leapt from him, the fire of goodness that had surrounded Magrell. He was aware of Magrell on his knees, seeing him through the mist that was all the sight he had left. Then Teon slipped into unconsciousness, his body unable to sustain him any more. Anga lifted him into her arms and with only the sounds outside, carried Teon to the door they had entered only twenty minutes before.

20

In the city the noise of the fire was growing. The city people could see the flames leaping high, see the smoke billowing into the sky, smell the smoke drifting over the city wall. The fire was incredibly fierce for those few minutes, and was leaping rapidly towards Durringham. Inside the walls of the city there were all sorts of reactions to the fire. Many of the refugees panicked, shouting, running around, particularly when the smoke began to enter the city sweeping through the streets. Many others, particularly those who lived in Durringham, realised that the flames would reach the city wall, but would go around the city – they always did. The soldiers in the city, both Fethonite and Bayronite, watched as children screamed, as some refugees ran in whatever direction they thought might be safe.

It was outside the city wall that the real but limited damage was being done by the fire. The tents of the Bayronite camp were quickly engulfed. The tents had been evacuated as the flames approached, so there were few casualties. But then the cart-drivers panicked. They mounted their carts and drove off to the West as quickly as possible running from the fire. They drove straight into the boggy ground to the North west of Durringham, an area the people called Kaylo's bog – named after a legendary giant who had attacked Durringham, and been caught in the bog and starved to death. The wheels of the carts were rapidly covered with mud; the oxen and carthorses quickly became stuck and bogged down. Within moments the Bayronite supply vehicles had been put out of use. The cart drivers made their way to the north side of the bog up to their knees in mud, escaping towards the Throneland. Most of the oxen and horses also escaped that way.

To the south of Durringham there were reserve troops, ready to join those in the city when the great banquet was over. They too wanted to avoid the flames, and saw safety only in the city. As the flames approached them they marched for the city, ran for the city. Within minutes the reserve troops had all entered the gates, as the flames leapt from patch to patch of heather or other dry vegetation, engulfing the area surrounding the city. As the flames reached the rhododendron bushes that surrounded the city they found new life and leapt on around the city walls.

Mayrog and his family stood on the hillside watching the fire. They had found Rayda, had bandaged her shoulder as best they could and lifted her carefully from the gully on a home-made stretcher, then carried her a little way down the road towards Durringham. They sat in amazement watching the plain in front of them. They had only lit a small fire which rapidly had engulfed the area. Earlier in the day the rain had fallen but had not really soaked into the plants, so that by eventide the heather had dried out again, tinder dry. They had watched the flames leap from their small fire to a patch of heather. Then from that patch to another and another, through the dry grass, through the small wooded copses in the area. Within half an hour the fire had completely surrounded Durringham. They all knew in reality that any fire damage would be superficial, would only make a small dent in the Bayronite effort, but it had made a good show. They could not believe the speed of what had happened. It was Mayrog who had spoken all their feelings. "This does not seem natural" he whispered. In spite of her pain Rayda whispered quietly. "It was what was needed".

In the banqueting hall there was uproar as the noise of the fire and smell of smoke became stronger. Some of the people panicked. The soldiers wanted to be outside: they didn't fight at dinner; they fought in the open with their men. The Bayronites rushed outside, began shouting to their fellow men. Those who kept a clear head began to put the mustering plan into action, calling the soldiers who had slipped into the city to the palace square with the simple code they had practiced and learnt in the afternoon. As their leaders began to cry "Bayronite to arms", so the cry swept through all the Bayronite soldiers, calling to each other "Bayronite to arms". At the cry to arms the Bayronite soldiers shed their cloaks and gathered in force in the square. Other soldiers, following their plan, had gathered at each of the gates. These groups at the gates were reinforced "accidentally" by the reserve troops who had fled into the city. It took little time for the Bayronites to have a complete grip of Durringham. All they had to do was sweep through the city from the centre, killing those who got in their way, forcing those who fled onto the swords of those who held the gates. It was clear – Durringham was theirs.

For Jayron there was only one thing to do – he wanted to be with his people. He knew the Bayronite troops were being mustered. He and his leaders knew that there would be no escape. He sent the message around the city through his army leaders that there was to be no fight. The King ordered his own soldiers to come to the square, that they would surrender with dignity. He had seen the events of the dining room, and somewhere still hoped against hope that something was happening, that a power beyond him was at work. He had returned inside the palace for a few moments to find the boy, the girl, whatever he could but there had been no time to search properly and they were nowhere to be seen – he had to be out in the square with his people.

Only Haren kept her head, perhaps the only person who understood what had happened, and she had one tool she could use – the messengers, the messengers she had persuaded Magrell to put in place. They would tell the story. She quickly went to the ante room where the messengers were assembled. She told them what had happened. Magrell had killed her husband. He had killed her son. He had unjustly invaded Fethon. That Magrell was no longer to be Emperor. Remarkably, no-one questioned – it seemed so obvious now. Haren ordered the messengers to go and tell. All the Bayronites, and as many other people as possible, had to know the truth. Quickly.

For some time in the city of Durringham there was pandemonium. The break-up of the great banquet. The mustering of forces. The arrival of the reserve troops. The panic of the refugees. The smell of the fire, the coughing and murkiness generated by the smoke. All added to the chaos. In the midst of the chaos there were snatched conversations. The beginning of rumours. The messengers at work. Word quickly spread of the events in the banqueting hall, the total defeat and discrediting of Magrell, the two young people who had turned the feast in less than ten minutes from Magrell's celebration to Magrell's humiliation. Hesteon, watching and listening, unable to move, quickly heard the rumours as he sat near the gate of the palace. He knew it could only be Teon and Anga. He also heard the terrible cost to the boy, how he had collapsed, and seemed totally lifeless. He had to go and find his son.

Hesteon looked around for something to help him, looked to the horses and saw Mayrog's staff that he had left behind. It was all he could find, so he pulled himself to his feet on the horse's stirrup and grabbed the staff. He tucked the staff under his arm, let go of the horse, and found himself standing balanced. He tried to move, using the staff as a type of crutch, and found it wasn't too difficult.

Hesteon moved towards the palace gates desperate to find his child, his son. Men were coming out of the gates, some rushing, some walking with dignity, both Bayronite and Fethonite. In the turmoil of the banqueting hall, and the smell of smoke, and the leaping flames no-one noticed a single man hobbling the other way. Hesteon slipped through the gate, then made his slow way hobbling towards the door. Here the rush through the door was greater, and Hesteon had to wait a few moments until he could enter the palace itself, squeezing between the door post and the soldiers leaving the palace.

The palace was like nothing Hesteon had ever seen before, so sumptuous, luxurious – though in reality much simpler and smaller than the Emperor's palace in Gresk – but only for a brief moment did Hesteon take notice. He saw someone who looked like a servant and hobbled over to him.

Hesteon grabbed the man's arm and asked him quickly. "Which way did the young people go"?

The servant, trying to leave the palace, pointed and answered quickly. "Through there. Through the banqueting hall. Out the other side." Hesteon released his arm and the servant rushed off.

Hesteon hobbled off in the direction the servant had pointed, hobbled through the dining hall, still in chaos as the diners had left so quickly. When he reached the great oak doors at the far end he struggled with the handles for a few moments, before pushing them open and walking through. He was in another corridor. Immediately he decided that he had to go left, but then right, no left. For a few moments Hesteon was uncertain which way he should go, then went with his original decision – left. He went along the corridor until it ended in a set of ornate marble stairs. He began to climb the stairs, slowly, hobbling between his stick and the banister rail. At the top he turned left and looked down another corridor. It was clearly an important part of the palace. This new corridor was wide, and along the walls were pictures of noble people, perhaps earlier kings. Suits of armour stood at intervals between the pictures. At the far end he saw light coming out through an open door, the only door that was open onto the corridor. The light seemed to call out to him. He began to hobble towards it, listening for anything that might come to him. Somehow he felt the open door held something, confirmed when he heard a sharp cry of fear come from the door. Hesteon was almost overtaken now in the panic to find his son, and the girl, who could be in that room. Another cry of fear: perhaps they were in trouble. He hobbled faster and faster down the corridor to the open door, hoping against hope....

At first the only person not to leave the banqueting hall was Magrell. After his encounter with Teon he had been left in a horrible mixture of feelings. Even when the hall had emptied he had been left kneeling on the floor. He had been humiliated. Totally humiliated. He knew that the boy had defeated him with a power he could not comprehend, a power greater than his own, and greater than the boy as well. Yet the conflict going on within him held him paralysed. On the one hand in the fire he had felt a power that could transform him. A power available to him that was greater than any power he had ever known before. On the other was the growing desire to hurt, to destroy, the desire that had grown since he had first killed the Emperor's son all those weeks back. Part of him wanted to give in to the power that the boy had shown him, but so much of him wanted to destroy, destroy the boy who had led to his humiliation. He remembered Hamlan, son of the Emperor, and the Emperor himself. He remembered the frenzied attack which he thought had killed the boy: he couldn't understand how he had survived. And the attack on Ganerr. He felt the power rising within him, the desire.... The desire for blood, the feelings of humiliation, the knowing there was someone stronger than him – all these came together to tip Magrell over the edge of sanity. He jumped to his feet, he pulled out his sword, he dashed for the door through which Anga and Teon had left a few minutes before. He would have the boy's blood. And the girl's blood. Or any blood.

Magrell dashed out into the corridor, turned left, searched the first room. He searched another – this time a store room. He ran along the corridor, up some stairs, into a bedroom – small – a servants room.

Then he saw more doors ahead. He tried one – it was locked. Another opened but no-one was there. Then, at the end of the corridor he spotted the door open, light flooding into the corridor. He knew – they were there. He did not know how, but knew – in that room he would find his quarry. Magrell walked slowly to the door, a triumphant look on his face, yet mixed with desire – his desire for blood. He reached the door and looked through. There on a bed he saw Teon lying, just conscious. Next to him Anga was sitting on the bed, mopping Teon's forehead with a damp cloth.

Magrell stood watching for what may have been two minutes, his bloodlust savouring the moment. Then he walked silently through the door and stood feet from the bed. He whispered very quietly. "Now I will finish you".

Both Anga and Teon looked at Magrell, his eyes glaring with anger and rage. Anga cried out in fear: they saw in him a fury they had never seen before in anyone. Magrell stood silently, sword in hand, ready to strike, the look on his face showing the enjoyment, the ecstasy of the moment. His face cracked in a smile, and he began to approach the bed slowly raising his sword above his head.

As he moved to the bed, Anga screamed again. Magrell leapt the last step, and he swung his sword hard. He would split Teon in two with one sweep – Teon had no escape. This surely was the end. Even Anga felt paralysed by the attack.

As the sword came down Magrell screamed out, lost his balance and fell to one side of the bed. The helmet from an old suit of armour had been hurled across the room at him, knocking him sideways just as he was about to strike. The sword plunged into the bed two inches from Teon's head. In the doorway stood Hesteon.

Magrell struggled to his feet, his fury even greater. He had forgotten Anga. He had forgotten Teon. There was only this idiot who had thwarted him. He looked at Hesteon, then rushed across the room towards him, sword raised. Before Hesteon or the others could move Magrell swung his sword. It cut deep into Hesteon's chest. He swung again, and again in his frenzy. Hesteon crumpled to the floor. The room was spattered with blood, covering not only Hesteon but Magrell himself, even being flung as far as Teon and Anga. Magrell was blind with rage. He swung his sword at the body now lying on the floor again and again. Repeatedly his sword plunged into the lifeless body at his feet. The blood flew from the blade. Hesteon did not know of this frenzied attack. He had died with the very first blow.

Magrell had run out of fury. His attack had subsided. Magrell's mind was clearing. He turned to the two young people. He spoke very quietly, coldly. "You have both caused me too much grief. You too must die". His words were suddenly lost as four men rushed into the room, knocked Magrell's sword from his hand, knocked him to the floor and held him there as he struggled and shouted. For minutes Magrell struggled and cursed. He cursed the soldiers, Jayron, Teon. He managed to kick one of the guards on the thigh.

At last Magrell's energy ran out, his struggles subsided. The men lifted him to his feet and led him out of the room.

Other soldiers came into the room and a Bayronite Sergeant spoke to Anga and Teon. "Please come with us". They lifted Teon very carefully and one of the soldiers took him in his arms. Anga followed behind with the sergeant and the other soldiers.

As they were mustered, the Bayronite's rapidly took control of the city. The leaders and Emperor's guard lined up in the square according to Magrell's earlier instructions. Other troops had secured the gates and roads into the city. The Fethonite people were still captive to fear, to the walls, to the soldiers, to the fire, unaware that Magrell was no longer at the head of the Bayronite forces. Jayron had also entered the square with his guard. He looked around and noticed one person missing: Magrell. Everyone else had gathered – the generals, the councillors, Haren. It was Haren who took control.

Since the events of the banqueting hall she had found new strength. She too had understood that this boy and the girl were very special. She too had begun to make sense of so much, made sense the horrors Magrell had committed over the last few weeks. She too had found the strength to ignore the letter – she would not be blackmailed any more, whatever the cost. She knew that this invasion of Fethon was wrong. In that hall she had discovered a power far greater than Magrell had ever shown. And Teon had hit her deep inside with the final words he had spoken: "I forgive you". Teon had a similar effect on many of the people there, particularly the Bayronites, showing them a dignity and honour that they had lost under Magrell, a dignity and honour they wanted restored to their people, to themselves. Even Jayron had not understood that part of Teon. He had seen the humiliation of Magrell. He had seen the power of Magrell over his people broken, but so transfixed had he been by these two young people, he had not seen the effect Teon and Anga had on others in the room.

Haren dismounted from her horse and walked over to Jayron. She invited him to meet with her and spoke quickly. "Sir, there is unfinished business before we can talk with you. We ask your indulgence, and ask that you give us time to sort these matters out".

Jayron realised he had little choice. He was still uncertain of the Bayronites although he could sense the change in the atmosphere. Should the Bayronites choose to enforce the wait he would have to wait, but he appreciated that Haren asked. Still deep down Jayron in confusion felt that this was the end, felt that within hours his country would be no more, his life would be no more. "Your majesty," He replied. "You must do as you see fit." Haren nodded and walked back to her troops and councillors. She gave orders that Magrell be brought to her, voluntarily or against his will, as quickly as possible. She knew she would not be disobeyed – the power that Magrell had over her people had been destroyed in the banqueting hall, and the rumours and messengers that had travelled around the city in half an hour had ruined his credibility with the common soldiers. She had given orders that the boy and girl be brought as well, that the soldiers take care of them.

It was Magrell who was brought first, covered in blood. The guards explained to Haren what had happened. Minutes later the other guards came, one carrying Teon who had sunk into semi-consciousness, another leading Anga gently by her hand. Anga herself felt almost totally paralysed by the horror of what she just witnessed. Hesteon had been her friend. Anga and Teon were both spattered with the blood from Magrell's frenzied attack.

Haren went across to Anga and spoke to her quietly. "Who was the man who died?" She asked.

At this Anga broke down in tears, the sheer emotion of everything, the last few days, the horrors she had seen, Magrell's brutality in the room, the death of a friend, all of this overwhelmed her. In the midst of her sobs, she spoke, one word at a time. "He Hesteon. He Teon's father." Haren put her arms around the girl as she sobbed uncontrollably. It was Jayron who walked across the square, put his robe on the ground then took Teon from the arms of the soldier and lay him on the robe. Jayron sat down as well and put his arms around Teon who had been roused out of his semi-consciousness when passed to Jayron. Tears rolled down Teon's face – he had no energy to cry any harder. Within moments Jayron too felt his own tears rising in his eyes, oblivious of the many soldiers formed up in the square.

With the sudden lull in activity, the people in the square were again aware that the fire in the heather had grown, having reached the Rhododendron's surrounding Durringham. There was a sudden gust of wind – so some thought – and the flames leapt high into the sky. Afterwards some said they had seen the face in the flames, the face of a child, a child with tears running down its face. Some knew that there was someone far greater, crying at their sorrow, crying at their pain, crying for the young people slumped in the square.

It was as Anga's sobs began to subside that riders came from the camp and reported to Haren what had happened in the fire: the Bayronite tents destroyed, the supply wagons stuck in the marshes.

Finally Haren, Anga, Teon and Jayron sat together on the floor in the middle of the square. Haren explained to Jayron what she knew of the events in the room a few minutes before. Haren was planning her speech – she now knew that she would have to take control of the Bayronites. Jayron wondering at these two young people who had suffered so much yet had used grace to save the country. Even the most hardened Bayronite felt touched by the presence of these four people. It was then they heard shouts.

Magrell had been standing between the guards watching all that had happened, disgusted and horrified that Haren was showing such a gentle attitude to the youngsters, to the Fethonites, disgusted that his own people gathered in that square had been drawn into what was happening with the four people in the centre. He also now understood the importance of the messengers, and the rumourmongers, that the soldiers would have talked to each other and all would have a picture of the defeat and humiliation of him: Magrell. Magrell knew that rumours would paint him in an even worse light than reality could. His mind, in hatred for those who had defeated him, shouted out, "Butcher them, butcher them". His hatred for Haren and Jayron, for Teon and Anga, multiplied in those few seconds. His loathing of the two youngsters was overwhelming.

As the four sat together in the square, he felt the soldiers guarding him relax slightly. He felt his guards lessening their concentration on him. He felt their guard lighten. Even in his fury, now multiplied by the desire for blood, more blood, Magrell's senses remained sharp, his cunning still at work.

Suddenly he struck out at one of the guards and knocked him to the floor. He grabbed the guard's sword and drove it into the thigh of one of the other guards who also crumpled to the floor, crying out in pain. He leapt out of the group of guards, dashed across the square to the four sat on the ground waving the sword he had grabbed, screaming "Bayron to arms" as he ran, trying to reach into the hearts of the Bayronites for one last time, trying to reach those who had earlier followed him blindly.

He screamed his hatred. He briefly saw that he was armed, the group of four were not. Within seconds he would reach them. They were defenceless. There was no-one close by to defend them. They would be dead. He was closing fast, ten yards, nine, eight, seven....

Suddenly Magrell screamed, staggered forward, stood for a few moments, then crumpled to the floor, his head resting on Teon's foot. From his back stuck a deeply embedded arrow, fired from the crowd of Bayronite soldiers. The soldier was never identified.

21

Magrell's body remained on the floor of the square. Haren asked Jayron to organise proper care for Teon. He and Anga were taken back into the palace and nurses sent for. In all that was happening earlier, Jayron had forgotten to get medical aid for Teon. As they were about to carry Teon from the square on a stretcher he raised his hand to stop them. His face was still stained with his tears and his father's blood. He still coughed every few moments. He looked to Haren and Jayron and whispered: "I still forgive him". As Teon was carried from the square, and as Anga walked with him, Haren's chief general, at her instigation, led three cheers that rang out around the square. Then Haren invited Jayron to stand with her, and spoke to the people gathered in the square.

"Friends, we now know the truth of recent events. We know that Magrell has killed both the Emperor and his son. We know that Magrell has caused a huge injustice to the Fethonite people. We know that we should not be here".

She turned to Jayron. "Sir, we have done you a great injustice. We are a noble people whose reputation was nearly destroyed by one man in his greed. We will repair any damage we may have done. And we will leave. Our hope is that we will be able to make peace between our two sister countries".

Jayron took his turn to speak. "Your majesty, we accept your apology, we can do no other: we have seen the two young people forgive far greater injustice. You and your people are welcome to stay here this night. We too look forward to building a relationship of trust and peace with your country."

Suddenly one of the Bayronite generals shouted: "Three cheers for Haren". The cheers that rang out broke the tension in the square as both Bayronite and Fethonite united in voice. There was no question now – Haren would take over leadership of her people.

22

Teon remained in the palace for several weeks recovering his health. The king's physicians set his broken arm properly, and the warmth of the palace allowed his chest time to heal and recover. Sadly, after the beating he had taken, three of his fingers – so badly broken they were beyond healing – had to be removed from the hand that was most badly injured. Only nature could heal the inner damage to Teon's health – the lungs, the internal bruising. The nurses had also washed him thoroughly, although he refused to let them remove his beard or cut his long hair. Anga found the period at the palace boring – there was little to do and she missed the mountains and forests, but in the early days she would not leave Teon, and nagged him to walk again, to eat, to talk. By the third week, Teon felt his arm was improving, had feeling and movement returning to damaged muscles, could stand alone and unaided, had regained some appetite.

Jayron visited regularly and oversaw the care Anga and Teon received in the palace. Anga and Teon's legend spread rapidly through the country. Teon lost none of the fire in his eyes that had developed over recent weeks, but spent much of his time lost in tears and sorrow, sorrow for Gowli, for his home, and mostly for his father. Other times he spent staring into space, overtaken by the trauma of what he had been through. Nights were often spent fighting off horrific nightmares, with fire trying to consume him, swords slashing in his direction.

During those early weeks a number of visitors came to see Anga and Teon, some staying at Jayron's palace for a few days. Some of the meetings had been heartbreakingly emotional.

Early in Teon's recovery Mayrog and Rayda were brought to Durringham escorted by Jayron's elite guard to be honoured by the king. It was Anga who met Mayrog and Rayda first. She felt nervous about meeting them: Anga remembered quite clearly that the last time she had seen Mayrog she had hit him over the head with a chair. A heavy wooden chair. She began to apologise in her north people way, noticing the gash on his forehead which she had obviously made, but was healing. At her apology Mayrog had burst out laughing. "No", he said. "The others wanted to string you up, but I thought you were about something far greater. You'll just replace the chair..." Again as Anga looked worried for a moment, Mayrog threw his head back and burst into laughter. He threw his arms around her, lifted her off the ground and hugged her harder than she had ever been hugged before. The three spent much of the day talking about what had happened.

Mayrog and Rayda also met Teon that evening – for most of the day he had been asleep or delirious. They hardly recognised him. Teon had been washed by the nurses and despite still being early days his health had improved so much: they realised they had only ever seen him briefly – for one night, when his health was as bad as it could be without him dying. They asked to be with him alone and Anga left them. Mayrog and Rayda sat on a couch with Teon lying in bed. After a while Mayrog spoke very quietly. "Teon, I ask your forgiveness. I left your father alone in the square. We could have stayed. Even one or two of us could have stayed. Your Father was my friend, although I didn't know he was your Father then. I am sorry at the horror of what you saw, I am sorry I did not do better."

Teon could say nothing – tears were filling his eyes yet again, and soon were streaming down his cheeks. Mayrog too shared in the tears, then Rayda. It was Teon himself who pulled them back together. He looked straight into Mayrog's eyes. Again Mayrog saw the fire that he had never seen before in anyone else. Teon spoke: "Mayrog, my friend", Mayrog noticed Teon's voice was getting stronger. "We will not talk of this again, you have nothing to regret." Mayrog looked into the eyes again and knew that Teon held nothing against him. His mind was pondering on this young man, and how such depth and wisdom lived in this still very frail frame.

Teon, however, hadn't finished speaking. "You too played your part, and paid your cost", he raised his good arm slightly and pointed at Rayda's heavily bandaged shoulder, the sling that held her arm, then pointed at Mayrog's scar before finishing his sentence: "and so I thank you". Suddenly Teon smiled in a way that Mayrog hadn't seen before, the smile of the fun-loving teenager Teon had once been. "Perhaps I'd better get you a helmet before she comes back...or remove the chairs..."

Messengers, accompanied by Anga herself – it was a break from the boredom of palace life – travelled to the North and found Anga's family: Comp, Angala, and Compson of the north people, the clan still staying at their southern campsite. There had been a hugely emotional reunion between Anga and her parents. As they travelled into Fethon at Jayron's invitation they caused much curiosity with their dark skins and wild appearance.

At the same time messengers travelled to Gresk at Teon's instigation. They were to invite Hansa to visit Teon.

The day that Teon, Anga, Hansa and the north people spent together passed in a mixture of laughter and tears, emotions running high in reunion between Angala and Hansa, and also between Teon and Hansa – it seemed an eternity since he had been at the commune. Jayron wisely excused himself "on business".

Six weeks after the end of the invasion Jayron arranged to spend time with Teon and Anga.

"Teon, Anga", he began gently. "I know it is still early days in your recovery, but it is time to talk about the future. As you know you are welcome to stay here as long as you wish. You saved our nation. However I need to ask: have you thought of what you might do next?"

As Jayron mentioned the future, it was the past: all that he had lost, that swept over Teon. His Father. Gowli. His home. Everything that had been taken away. Teon began to sob in tears – it was only six weeks earlier that he had seen his father murdered and the wounds still pierced him deeply. As his tears fell, and still suffering the effects of the physical battering he had taken over those weeks, Teon looked incredibly vulnerable. Wounded in spirit, his vulnerability was emphasised as the cough returned for a moment. As he wept, so Anga and Jayron shed tears as well.

At last Teon pulled himself together. His voice was still rough from the chest problems he had though the cough was pretty well gone. He began to speak.

"I have spent much time talking to him". His hand pointed to a candle in the room, then pointed to his own face. "I have spent much time listening to him as well and I believe this is what he wants. He wants me to go and live in Golo, on the high plateau. He wants us to be a place where all people's can gather. He wants us to maintain his worship in the midst of the people. He wants us to be the guardians of his words and presence. We will go to Golo."

There was no arguing with Teon when he spoke, and his words were greeted with silence. It was Jayron who broke the silence. "Teon, the choice is yours, and if that is what you want, then so be it." Jayron hesitated, then spoke affectionately. "But, lad, you are still in a bad way both physically and spiritually. It will take you many months to recover. The high plateau is not a good place in your condition." Again the room was quiet.

Again Teon spoke: "I have thought about this as well, and have spoken to Mayrog. And to Comp. And to Hansa. Until we are ready to move to Golo we will stay with Mayrog and his family. We will stay in their settlement and prepare for the final part of the journey. Comp and his family have agreed to prepare Golo for us. Some of the ladies at Hansa's commune are already preparing to join us."

The most puzzled and animated face of all belonged to Anga who had remained silent until this moment. She burst in: "He speak. He say us. Who us? Who else at Golo?"

Teon smiled again the youthful teenager smile. He replied: "Me and my wife".

Anga was still agitated. "You no wife. You alone. You tell me." Teon held up his hand to stop Anga's flow.

Teon looked to Jayron and spoke. "Sir, as king you are allowed to perform marriages. Will you please marry Anga and me".

Anga got to her feet, her anger rising. She shouted at Teon. "You ask. No ask me. Ask me first".

Teon smiled again as he held up his hand. He spoke quietly. "I'm sorry Anga, I was lost in my ideas. Will you marry me?"

160

Anga looked like she was about to explode as she stood before Teon. She looked around and saw the glass on the table beside her. She picked the glass up, took two steps towards Teon and threw the contents – thankfully water, unfortunately cold – straight into Teon's face. Teon had a look of shock as the cold water dripped onto his clothes. Anga turned to Jayron. She spoke forcefully: "Now. King. We will marry."

The marriage was Teon's first appearance in public after the invasion of the Bayronites. Rumours about him circulated; stories of his prowess were widespread. What had happened at the great feast was talked over by everyone. He had grown bigger and stronger and mightier and more handsome with every day of rumour. No-one stayed at home for the wedding – Teon was by now a national folk hero – yet only a few people had any sense of what he was like or even what he looked like. Anga too had entered people's hearts for her support for Teon, but she had been seen often in the streets of Durringham. No-one was quite prepared for the slim sickly unkempt youth, his hair uncut, his beard growing in length but no thicker, simply dressed in black trousers and dark red smock – he had refused everything grander that Jayron had tried to get him to wear. Teon was still uncertain on his feet and walked with a stick to help him. The real Teon caused even more rumour and conversation than the romantic figure so many had created. Teon's simplicity was in hugely marked contrast to the massive crowds, the welcome, the cheering, the celebrations.

The wedding ceremony was very simple, performed by Jayron in the early afternoon. By mid-afternoon Teon and Anga were leaving Durringham in Mayrog's cart – they had refused every other form of transport, every other gift that the people of Durringham wanted to give them. The mystery of these young people was just beginning in the minds and hearts of the Fethonites.

In Golo a candle was burning. The face in the candle-flame smiled....

Printed in the United Kingdom
by Lightning Source UK Ltd.
9805900001BA/1-18